BOOK ONE: THE WAY OF THINGS

Giants in the Land

CLARK RICH BURBIDGE

Illustrated by Karl C. Hepworth

Giants in the Land, Book One: The Way of Things

© 2012, 2023 Clark Rich Burbidge
© 2012, 2023 Illustrations by Karl C. Hepworth

Published by
Clark Rich Burbidge
Woods Cross, Utah
www.giantsinthelandbook.com

Platformed by Ingram Spark

Book ISBN—13: 9798218165192, EBook ISBN - 13: 9798218165185

Library of Congress Control Number: 2020943501

Printed in the USA

To my Sweetheart, Leah,
And all the other "Giants" in my life.

Other Books
by Clark Rich Burbidge

Fiction: Gold Medal Award-Winning Young Adult Series:

StarPassage: Book One – The Relic
StarPassage: Book Two – Heroes and Martyrs
StarPassage: Book Three - Honor and Mercy
StarPassage: Book Four - Cyber Plague

Fiction: Gold Medal Award-Winning Young Adult/Middle Reader Trilogy:

Giants in the Land: Book One – The Way of Things
Giants in the Land: Book Two – The Prodigals
Giants in the Land: Book Three – The Cavern of Promise

Fiction: Gold Medal Award-Winning Family Christmas Picture:

A Piece of Silver: A Story of Christ

Non-Fiction: Gold Medal Award-Winning Family/Personal:

Living in the Family Blender:
10 Principles of a Successful Blended Family

Life on the Narrow Path: A Mountain Biker's Guide to Spiritual Growth in Troubled Times

Websites:

"http://www.starpassagebook.com" www.starpassagebook.com
"http://www.giantsinthelandbook.com"
www.giantsinthelandbook.com
"http://www.apieceofsilver.com" www.apieceofsilver.com
Like my Facebook page and catch all the news at:
www.facebook.com/clarkrburbidge
www.facebook.com/blendedfamilyproject

CONTENTS

Author's Note

IT HAS BEEN AN AMAZING ride to produce my first fiction chapter book. The need for characters and settings with depth and richness requires a dramatic change in approach and research. It first involved creating the basic characters and storyline. Then—by filling in the details—the reader steps into the story and lives it with the characters, rather than just reading along.

Giants in the Land emphasizes key character traits critical to help cope with life's sudden changes, particularly with the loss of, or separation from, loved ones. It presents truth in a way that captivates young people as well as adults as they personally identify with the characters.

It is the nature of humankind to seek out individuals and circumstances as examples. Such influences teach us how to confront sudden change or find security in difficult times. After following for a lifetime in another's footsteps, we may look back with surprise as we discover how many walk in *ours*. The responsibility may be overwhelming, but it cannot be sidestepped. We must carry on, doing the best we can and hoping it is enough. *Giants in the Land* gives readers of all ages insight into why and how becoming something more than they have been can be so important.

It is my hope that all who enter this land will discover what it means to have the heart of a giant and find hope and new meaning in life. This is, after all, The Way of Things.

GIANTS
in the
LAND
Village
Port
Western
Lands

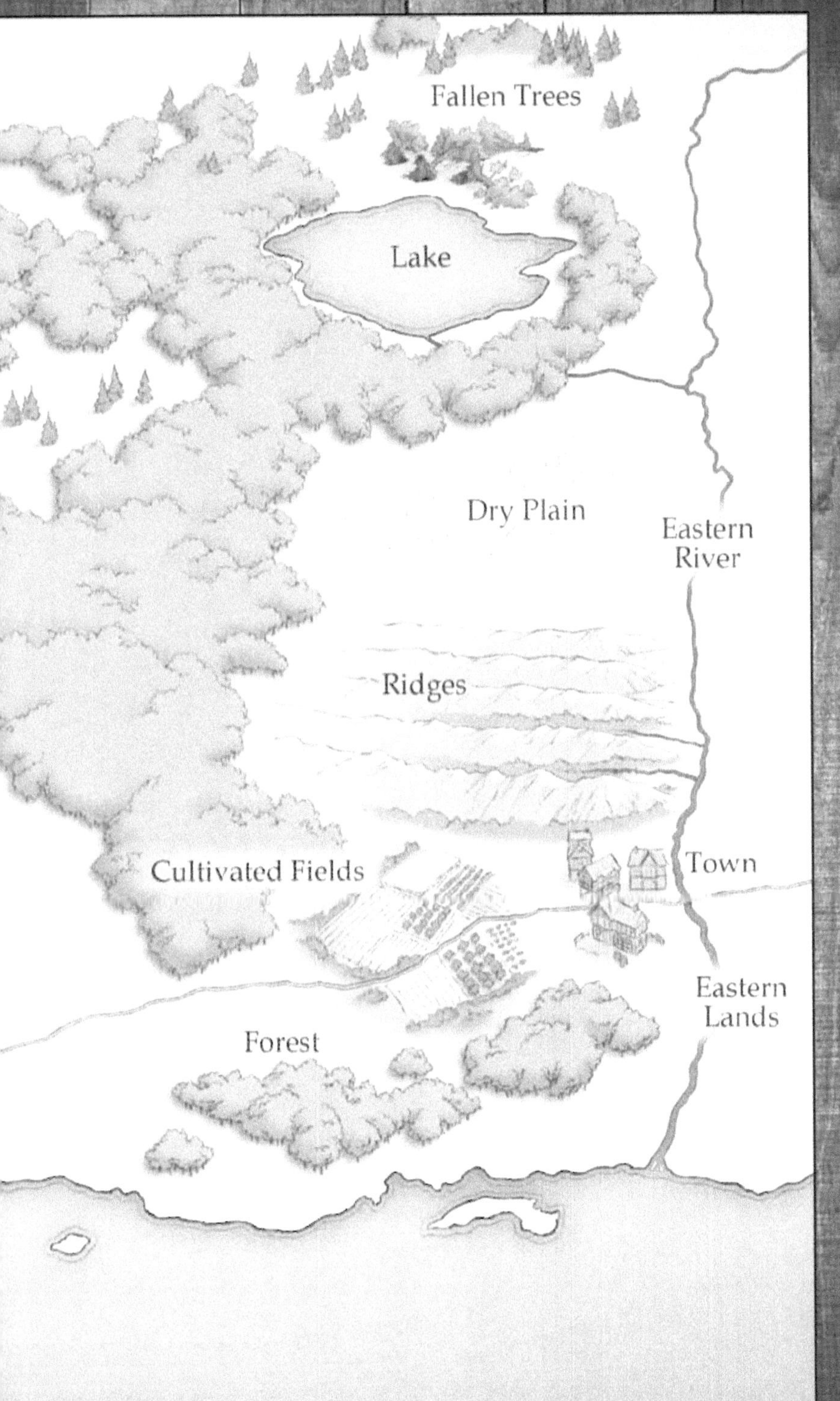

Fallen Trees
Lake
Dry Plain
Eastern River
Ridges
Cultivated Fields
Town
Eastern Lands
Forest

Prologue

Shadow in the Woods

AIDEN HAD RUN FOR MILES. His sixteen year old legs burned with pain as he scrambled through the woods. He desperately needed to rest but he dare not stop. It had rained most of the day in the foothills, delaying his departure and making the ground muddy and slippery. His pace had slowed but his muscles were driven onward by his will. Aiden was large for his age and crashed through limb and branch, no longer concerned about stealth. Everything depended on making it to the hidden dugout canoe. He could hear the rushing of the western river in the distance, just a little farther he told his failing legs.

He and his father had prepared several weeks for the dangerous journey. His mother was due to give birth any day so his father was unable to accompany him. He was the one chosen anyway and was ready to do all he could. Strict secrecy had been kept. But somehow word of the journey had come to the ears of the Mayor. The carefully laid plan was in tatters and he was in a mad dash for his life. Aiden felt sure he was being followed. The men behind him were relentless. They moved in nearly perfect harmony with the sounds of the forest. Few would have known they followed, but they were there. The dark haired boy had hunted all his life and could feel it.

Somehow the mayor knew and had placed his best trackers on the edge of town. Aiden was fortunate to see them first and skirt their camp. With the immediate danger past he grew careless and slipped on a mossy root. His rucksack banged against the trunk of a tree echoing through the forest. The men knew the sound and flew toward him.

Aiden was clever and had backtracked twice to throw them off. But he felt the men closing the distance as he approached the river. "How could they have known?" he thought out loud.

The Mayor has eyes and ears everywhere in town. There are few that would not inform for a few pennies, his thoughts came back. Aiden prayed that his parents and unborn sibling would be safe.

With a pounding heart he broke into a clearing near the river bank. He quickly uncovered the canoe and pulled it toward the river. A crack of a branch came from behind. "Ee's over 'ere!" came a call followed by feet crashing through the underbrush from several directions. "We ain't gonna 'arm ya, boy!" came a voice from another direction. Aiden shoved the canoe toward the center of the stream and jumped aboard. It was light enough to skim upriver against the strong current. Looking back he saw several large rough looking men with clubs and knifes burst out of the forest. *At least there were no bowmen,* he thought. He was safe for now.

He turned upstream and could barely keep pace with its swift flowing current. Paddling with all his might he moved north toward its headwaters. He angled toward the far side of the river to reach safety and escape the swift current. Each stroke caused the canoe to lurch forward as he strained with every sinew.

He glanced at the bank behind. Shadows were moving through the edge of the forest keeping pace. He had not intended to fight the main current but had no choice. The rain had swollen the river and filled it with potentially deadly debris. Trunks and tree branches were the most dangerous. He stroked and dodged for about a mile until he reached calmer water near the right bank and began to move more swiftly. *My pursuers cannot possibly cross to this side until the ford which is another two miles farther up,* he thought to himself. *This should be safe while I catch my breath.*

But the boy was wrong. Ten minutes after reaching the far side of the river he again heard crashing steps in the forest just out of sight. They were coming from his side of the river and he saw an enormous shadow passing through the trees. There was nothing left to do but move out into the current again.

Aiden steered the canoe toward the center around logs and boulders. As he reached the middle of the river he looked back at the right bank and saw a tall thin creature step from the forest. The creature was above twenty feet in height and gestured wildly pointing upstream. The boy was in shock at the sight and turned his attention, too slowly, to look upstream. A large uprooted trunk was bearing down on him at great speed. He paddled with mighty strokes to get out of the way but was caught fully sideways by the trunk.

The canoe snapped in half dumping him into the frigid water. He struggled against the rushing current before being sucked into a whirlpool on the downstream side of a huge boulder. Aiden had a brief glance at the near bank. The tall creature was running along the bank in his direction. He felt himself swirling in circles as the river reached out its deadly embrace. He had failed in his attempt to get help for his people. He hoped another could take his place. The cold unforgiving fingers wrapped him in their final caress and his mind went dark.

The long-expected journey began in the dark of the night. Dozens of shadows moved silently under a full moon. A heavy tap on a resting shoulder, a kick of a booted foot, and they were on the move. Soundlessly, they fell into a long, ragged line stretching north. They knew they would never see their lifelong friends again. It was a solemn march, with each one of the travelers left to his or her own concerns about the difficulties they would leave in their wake.

A lonely figure trailing at the end of the line hesitated and looked back . . . one last time. She cast an immense shadow in the moonlight. A second larger shadow approached. The moon shone brightly on his wavy red hair.

"It is always hardest the first time, but it never becomes easy," he said.

"Why must we leave?" asked the smaller shadow. "They trusted us. They will never understand."

Placing a steadying hand on her shoulder, the larger shadow answered, "It is not for us to decide how they will feel. That is part of the purpose here. We have completed our task and, as you know, there are others."

"Yes, I know it is time, but my heart remains heavy," the smaller shadow said with a catch in her voice.

The larger shadow turned toward the north. "They will be all right after a time," he whispered. "They have The One among them. He does not yet understand, of course, for he must travel a long and difficult path to discover himself. That is The Way of Things."

There was nothing more to say. The two shadows turned their backs on the valley they had served for many lifetimes and disappeared forever over the northern ridge.

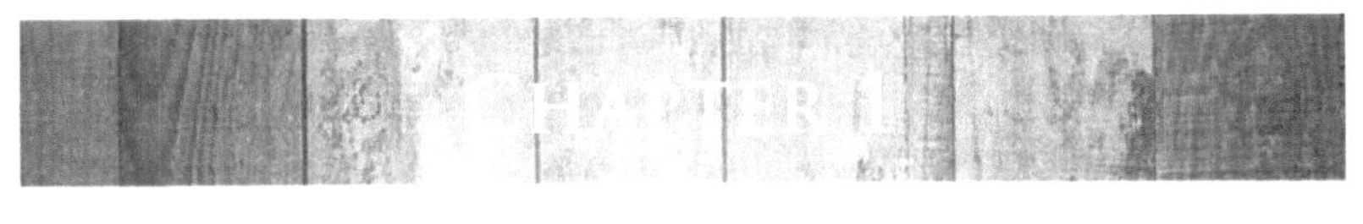

Giants in the Land!

THE PANIC BEGAN as the sun rose over the levee on the banks of the great eastern river. It struck each of the townsfolk who were arriving for work in the wheat fields at the same moment. It was a mindless, helpless panic, brought on by sudden, unexpected events. From the fields, the panic spread through town like a disease for which there was no cure. The captain and his guard were immediately called out.

The news hit the first homes like a tidal wave, tearing at lives that could not comprehend the attack. Fear gripped each man and woman; children were in tears at the loss. The flood continued down each quiet street and shook the foundations of each home. No one was spared.

Townsfolk fell to their knees in desperate prayer. The rising tide of panic rushed up to the door of each home. Remorseless and unforgiving in its progress, none went untouched.

The fruits of fear borne on the shoulders of these floodwaters consumed each home and its inhabitants without warning, until the flow lapped at the flagstone steps of a small cottage near the northern edge of town. There it waited hungrily for the door to open so it could consume another victim. It lay unseen and unexpected as those inside prepared for a day that could not be prepared for. Inside the cottage, a young man rose early and readied himself for the day. He had no idea that today everything he knew would change forever.

Barely into his twenties, Thomas was strong and agile. His blond hair hung slightly over his ears and was unkempt from the night's rest. The face that looked back at him from the mirror was handsome but already carried the careworn lines of great responsibility and a life of unrelenting hard labor. His deep blue eyes were alert and watchful, and betrayed the secret of his youth. Even as a lad he could spy a hawk far off in the sky long before anyone else. He was attentive and hardly ever missed a detail as he measured and cut, plowed and planted.

Thomas raised his hands to his face. His hands were strong and calloused and his finely muscled arms had been sculpted by many years of work in the fields and forests. But scars came from such a life. One scar under his chin from a fall as a youth; a more recent and serious one still healing on his back. It had come from that terrible day six months ago when a newly cut tree had fallen the wrong way and had nearly taken his life.

Thomas poured water from the pitcher into a basin and washed his face and hands. His wife, Rachael, had thoughtfully heated the water and left it for him. Its warmth helped cast aside the last few scales of sleep. As the young man looked in the mirror, he thought about his father, who had passed away six months before. That was the day everything had changed for Thomas.

I miss his advice, his guidance, and his friendship, he thought. An only child, he had grown up laboring in the fields and forests alongside his father. They had walked hand-in-hand and then side-by-side to the fields countless times. His father had taught him many skills necessary to hunt, using the great yew bow that hung above the hearth. At a young age, Thomas became the first of his peers to draw the powerful bowstring to his right ear. He was also a skilled tracker and could approach even the wariest of forest creatures soundlessly.

Thomas had also been instructed in the times and seasons for successful farming. He knew how to read the skies and the lengthening or shortening of days to know when to plant or gather each crop. He learned the value of preparing early for winter. He exercised patience and attention to detail in keeping the rows clear of weeds and vermin in order to bring in a large harvest. *You could have taught me so much more, Father, but our time together was cut short.*

Then the thought came to him again, as it had on so many other mornings: *How could a loving god have allowed such an important part of my life to be taken?* He couldn't help recalling that terrible accident. As the tree lay across his father's broken body, Thomas had overlooked his own deep wound. He had cried a deep, soul-rending cry, familiar to any who have suffered a loss that changed their life instantly and forever. He remembered trying to lift the tree until others arrived to help.

Thomas would have gladly exchanged places with the life that was taken, but it had not been his decision to make. The long scar on his back reminded him how God could watch over and protect. At the same time, however, it was a warning that life was fragile and could change in an instant.

Thomas was not ungrateful or bitter. He had a good life and considered himself blessed and happy. He had a beautiful young family, work that made a difference, and a closeness he felt to his God. Yet, a dull pain always seemed present. There remained an empty place in his heart that could not be filled. He longed for just one more good conversation with his father.

These were feelings he did not know how to talk about with his wife, or with anybody else. He locked them away in his heart, tried to focus on the day's work, and bore his burden alone. There is no reason to struggle over this, he told himself. He and his father had enjoyed a great relationship. There were no unresolved arguments or hard feelings; no unfinished business. Yet, he felt his life had been robbed of something priceless that could not be recovered. Someday soon, he hoped his burden would begin to ease.

His morning preparations complete, Thomas walked down the wood-hewn hallway. As he passed an opening in the center of the wall, he looked in on his sleeping daughter. "Hope," he whispered softly as he did each morning, "I love you, my little sweetheart. I am always here for you."

Thomas thought of his father's joy when his only granddaughter had been born two years before. It was as if this young child had filled his heart after so many years of emptiness following his own wife's passing of a winter disease few had understood. Hope's birth was a joyous moment. She had a way of bringing light to every room she entered with her white-blond hair and round, smiling face.

Thomas felt better and headed down the narrow, winding stairway to the main floor. Rachael had made biscuits, and their fresh, warm aroma wafted from the kitchen. He passed into the common room, which was dominated by a great river-stone fireplace smelling of burnt wood. His gaze fell upon the bow, quiver of arrows, and hunting knife hanging above it on the soot-stained wooden wall. They had been handed down from father to son for a hundred years and had become his at his father's passing.

He continued to the kitchen, where the smell of biscuits beckoned. Rachael, her auburn hair falling across her shoulders, greeted him with a warm embrace. They enjoyed their brief, quiet moment together. They were not husband and wife merely by chance or convenience. The couple remained deeply in love and devoted to the joy they had found together.

Their life was menial and hard, but Thomas always marveled at the way Rachael could do so much with such limited resources. This morning was no exception. Their circumstances made for a somewhat meager breakfast, but they were both happy and filled.

Thomas lingered a bit longer than usual, talking about the day with his dear wife. Then he kissed her and walked toward the front door of their humble cottage. Rachael called him back and extended her hand. In it lay one freshly cut wildflower from the garden.

She wished him well and laid its delicate yellow petals and stem in his hand. "This is to remind you that Hope and I will be here this evening to welcome you to a warm hearth," she said.

It was amazing how Rachael always said the right thing when he was feeling burdened. He knew she could read his feelings. Thomas appreciated it when, without a word, Rachael did something like this to bring new light into his life. His painful thoughts evaporated as he gazed into her deep brown eyes. Her eyes looked beautiful in the morning light pouring through the east-facing kitchen window.

Thomas kissed her again, longer this time. Then he shouldered his bag, in which Rachael had packed some extra biscuits and venison, and turned to face the day. He moved purposely through the cottage door and down the dirt walkway toward his small front gate. There was much on Thomas' mind, and he paid little attention to his surroundings. *I need one, perhaps two more days to finish clearing the rocks, trees, and stumps from the field*, he mused, deep in thought. The new acreage required planting, and the growing season had already begun. *Hopefully, the blacksmith has repaired my plow.* It had been severely damaged when it hit a large, buried boulder.

"My father," he murmured aloud, "would have the field planted by now." Thomas had his father's and grandfather's name. He knew he must carry it well in honor of those who had gone before as well as for those who would come after.

It was true that the work before him today would be difficult. He had some catching up to do, but he knew it would get done . . . *for there were giants in the land!*

Yes, there really were giants in the land! That fact was as true as the blue sky above and as constant as the river running by to the east. Giants were as much a part of daily life as the shoemaker's shop across the road.

No one remembered how or when the giants first arrived. Perhaps they had always been here; perhaps not. But such thoughts were unimportant. Thomas knew, as had his father, that life in their village had changed little over the years. There were some things one could always rely on, and the most important of these were the giants.

The townsfolk and the giants had a wonderful relationship. The giants dug canals for irrigation, built and maintained the levee that protected the town from flooding, and removed stumps and large boulders from the fields. They plowed, quarried the ore for the blacksmith's forge, carried heavy stones for foundations and fences, and prepared and placed the long lengths of timber for homes and shops.

The townspeople relied heavily upon the giants. Planting and harvesting went smoother, and wolves and bears did not roam the valley. The giants' presence kept them away. Roads and bridges were smooth, wide, and kept in good repair. Life in the town was better and easier because of the giants.

The giants had nearly completed a walled fortress for the people's protection and support in times of need. It was not a castle, but more of a stockade, with grain silos and a high, strong rock wall. "Why do the giants think such a fortress is necessary?" Thomas and the other townsfolk often wondered aloud.

True, bands of robbers roamed the wild world and preyed upon innocent travelers or unprepared villages. The townsfolk had heard enough stories, so they knew it was true. But what could threaten their valley that the giants couldn't handle and a fortress could? The people gave little thought to the dangers around them because, in their opinion, there were no real threats. They had their giants.

No one knew where the giants went at night, and few cared. The village homes were strong and safe, and the giants always returned in the morning. At night, the giants also left a lookout on the northern ridge. The people rarely attempted to travel beyond the river and the ridge. When travel *was* necessary—like to the western quarries or mines—a giant companion always accompanied them.

The villagers had few needs and the world, after all, was a dangerous place. When the giants departed each evening, the town grew quiet. The townsfolk did not venture far from their shops and homes after dark. They warmed themselves at their hearths and were content with their lives.

Many citizens spent their days displaying their wonderful skills in crafting furniture, rope making, shoemaking, and dressmaking. The blacksmith was well-known for the quality of his workmanship. People came from miles around to sample the delicious goods from the baker and the chocolatier. The town also boasted its share of fine guildsmen, tradesmen, and artisans. Instructors of renown dutifully taught the children their letters, history, and herb lore.

The giants were not slaves. True, they did the heavy lifting, but it was not as if the townsfolk did not contribute. They built, planted, and harvested like people in any town. They treated the giants with respect and honor as they worked side by side with their towering friends. Thomas certainly could not have built his cottage in one season had it not been for the giants' help in laying the foundation, log frame, and roof.

The giants not only did things for the people that they could not do for themselves, but they also deeply affected how the townsfolk felt about themselves and their belief that nothing could upset their lives.

The people went about their daily activities with the confidence that whenever they came upon a job too large, an obstacle too heavy, or a threat too great, the giants would step in. The townsfolk knew in their hearts that the giants would always be there to make things run smoothly.

However, a storm of change was already upon them that would soon test their very souls.

Something Wrong

THE TOWNSFOLK AND the giants had always lived together in peace and harmony. Both could not imagine a happier time. Thomas knew this as he walked out the door. He was filled with the same confidence he felt every day. But as he approached the front gate, he noticed something very different. The town was in an uproar. Townsfolk rushed to and fro. Shock and fear showed on their faces as they hurried past.

This never happeneds! Thomas thought in alarm. He caught hold of the baker and asked, "What is going on?"

The baker stopped only long enough to exclaim, "What shall we do? How will I get wheat to bake my bread if the fields cannot be cleared, planted, and harvested?" He shook off Thomas' hold and scurried away.

Thomas stepped out into the street. The captain of the guard galloped up on his great, white stallion. The horse reared in front of Thomas, forcing the young man to dive into the bushes to avoid being trampled.

"Out of my way!" the captain cried, reigning in his horse only slightly. "The fortress wall is not complete and the granaries are unfilled! How will we protect ourselves in this dangerous world?"

What is the matter? Thomas wondered, confused. As he stood and brushed himself off he noticed the hulking figure of the blacksmith lumbering by. Thomas tried to stop him, but the blacksmith brushed him aside.

"No coal for the fires, no iron for the blades, what to do, what to do?" the large man mumbled repeatedly without noticing Thomas.

Thomas looked around for someone who could tell him what was happening. He noticed the shoemaker's head popping up and down in his shop window across the street. Thomas approached him. Perhaps he would know why the town was in such an uproar.

"Sir," he pleaded, "What is wrong with everybody this morning?"

"They're gone," the shoemaker said in a shaky voice and ducked back down.

"*Who* is gone?" asked Thomas, exasperated.

"The giants . . . they're gone," came the frightened response from below the windowsill.

Thomas was stunned into disbelieving silence. Then gathering his wits, he asked, "All of them?"

The shoemaker peered out again. "Yes, every one of them."

Thomas kept his voice calm. "This cannot be," he reasoned. "Where did they go?"

"The captain and his guard have searched the countryside from river to ridge, but there is no trace of them. Oh, what shall we do? We are doomed!" The shoemaker slammed the shutters closed and disappeared into the dark recesses of his shop.

Alarmed at this news, Thomas hurried out to his fields. Only yesterday, he and one of the giants had been clearing trees and boulders from the land. Now, he found the work as he had left it the evening before. He had worked for many years with this particular giant, a broad-shouldered, red-haired, soft-spoken behemoth who called himself Forestmaster.

Thomas believed the giant was honest and faithful and would never abandon the people. He trusted Forestmaster, who was also his closest friend. *If I can find Forestmaster, I know he will provide the answers to this mystery,* he mused. Forestmaster seemed to be a leader among the giant people. Thomas looked across his land, but there was no sign of the red-headed giant. *How can this be?* He called out and searched, but there was no answer.

The fields before him lay ghostly quiet in the morning mist. Thomas was confused by the events of the morning and needed to keep a clear mind. Fear crept into the edges of his thoughts. Panic solves nothing, he reminded himself. He mouthed a brief prayer asking for strength and wisdom as he struggled to understand what had happened and how to respond.

Then Thomas raised his head. The answers would not to be found in the fields this day. He also realized that if the giants had indeed left, his own work could not continue without many helping hands. So he turned for home, his mind filled with questions.

As he approached the town, Thomas noticed a crowd gathered at its northern end. He worked his way to the front to see what had attracted their attention. It was a large crowd, and Thomas had to climb on a watering trough to get a good look.

From his perch, Thomas could see far beyond the crowd. He noticed many individual trails coming together. They formed one enormously wide path of huge footprints leading up and over the nearby hills. This expanse of trodden-down grain and shrubbery could only have been made by the departing giants.

"Well," the baker said angrily, "we don't know why, but we can see which direction they went."

Curious, Thomas jumped down from the trough and followed the giants' path for almost a mile. *How could this have happened?* he wondered. *More importantly, why did they leave?* The trail led straight to the hills and disappeared over the first northern ridge. As he walked, Thomas fell into deep thought in an attempt to retrace his interactions with Forestmaster and the other giants over the past few days. He needed to determine if there was anything in the giants' behavior that might have signaled their disappearance.

Forestmaster was in a jolly mood yesterday, Thomas remembered. The giant's hearty, booming laugh never failed to shake the forests and lift Thomas' spirit. Their conversation had revolved mostly around work and their good fortune in having such splendid and talented wives. Forestmaster was particularly proud of his wife Threadweaver's work with cloth and hides. He proudly showed Thomas his new leather belt, decorated with finely ornate carvings, as evidence of her skill.

Rachael had thoughtfully slipped some extra biscuits into Thomas' pack, which he had shared with Forestmaster. "Truly worthy of a giant's kitchen!" Forestmaster had pronounced. That was high praise.

Was there something more Forestmaster wanted to tell me yesterday? Thomas asked himself. *Had he missed something in the giant's deep green eyes? A flash of regret perhaps?* No, it was just his overactive mind looking for something when there was nothing.

He recalled Forestmaster waving to the giant Stonebreaker, who had come to collect a pile of wagon-sized boulders from Thomas' field. "These will be excellent for use in the fortress walls," Forestmaster had remarked, looking pleased.

Had Stonebreaker seemed untypically somber at the time? Could it simply have been the heat of the day or the burden of work that occupied the giant's mind? Stonebreaker was a practical joker and always had something clever or witty to share. But there had been no conversation with him yesterday, just a wave of his hand.

What about last night? Thomas thought back carefully. *Was there anything unusual about my parting with Forestmaster?* He did remember that when he'd said, "See you tomorrow," Forestmaster had already turned and was walking away. *Had he failed to hear my farewell? Or . . . was he hiding something? Might I have seen a clue in his face if Forestmaster had not turned away?*

Thomas had made a habit of observing and making note of details. However, what he had seen yesterday was of no help to him now. He could think of nothing in his interactions with the giants that could have foretold this troubling event.

Looking back, there may have been subtle clues that only now seemed meaningful. But none shed any light on the current situation, and Thomas saw that his friends and neighbors were wild with panic and fear.

What to Do?

WHEN THOMAS RETURNED to town he discovered that the mayor had called a town meeting for that very hour. He arrived a few minutes late and found mass confusion. The mayor was pounding his gavel to bring everyone to order, but his efforts were overwhelmed by the wailing and anxious conversation of a hundred voices.

Thomas found Rachael and Hope near the back of the throng. He tried to tell them what he had seen, but he could scarcely be heard over the tumult. Finally the noise diminished enough for the meeting to be called to order.

Mayor Nimblebone was tall and thin, almost to the point of looking ill. His clothes hung on him as if made for a man twice his size. His wide flat-brimmed hat fluttered in the wind and wobbled every time he slammed the gavel down on the wooden platform. Had the situation not been so serious, Thomas would not have been alone in finding humor at the sight.

The moment was far from humorous, however. Mayor Nimblebone was a good, honest man in an impossible situation. Living with giants had solved many problems and eliminated most crises, with the exception of the passing of loved ones. The mayor had never faced a problem such as he had been thrust into today and he appeared to be at a loss about where to begin. He allowed some of the people to express their concerns.

Several lined up on the platform and addressed their friends and neighbors. Thomas had heard the same questions spoken in the streets earlier. Apparently, there were still no answers. Desperation edged many of the comments. Some people had specific problems or obstacles that they said they could not overcome without the giants' help. Others expressed their fear and dread and stated they could not function at all.

Everyone sought answers to the common questions: Why did the giants leave, and where did they go? Although there were no solutions, the opportunity to speak provided an outlet for some of their greatest fears. It calmed the people to know they were all in this calamity together.

Once those who felt a need to speak finished, the mayor asked for ideas to address specific needs. "There are things that must be done, and we need everyone's help," he said. "I have here a list of tasks that are most in need. We will review the list, and the clerk will write the names of volunteers to help complete each task. Come now. We can do this if we work together."

Volunteers stepped forward to resolve many of the most urgent needs. Many agreed to go into the fields and harvest the ripest of the crops to save them before the rains came. The river levee needed to be completed, and a large group formed to help with that. Although they could not determine how to move the massive boulders into place, several skilled masons volunteered to assist with temporary work to complete the fortress walls.

Thomas knew it was good that the townsfolk had addressed some of the most urgent matters. However, he noticed that a surprisingly large number of his friends and neighbors seemed unable to act. They looked paralyzed with fear and dread. As the same questions kept surfacing over and over the lack of answers seemed to drive them deeper into hopelessness, robbing them of their will to move forward.

The questions continued: "Where have the giants gone?" "Why did they leave?" "Will they return?" "Did someone offend the giants, causing their departure? If so, who is to blame?" Most of all, they asked, "What do we do now?"

It was obvious the people needed answers to these questions, in order to bring the full resources of the town into action again. "We must send a troop of hearty souls in search of the giant people," announced the captain of the guard.

"But they must not be compelled!" the blacksmith said loudly. "Only a voluntary commitment from the heart will be sufficient for the perilous journey ahead."

Mayor Nimblebone quickly agreed. "Their goal will be to find the giants *and* to bring them back!"

The entire crowd gave a great *hurrah* and threw their hats in the air.

The mayor, seeming pleased at the way his statement had roused the crowd, continued, "Who among you will step forward on this great quest for town and people, for wife and family, for life itself?" He was on a roll now. His gift had always been the turn of a phrase and his ability to emotionally move a crowd.

Surely, many will be moved by his speech and step forward! Thomas thought.

To his surprise, the cheers trailed off and the crowd became deadly silent. They waited to see who would be the first to step forward. But they waited in vain. Not a single person answered the mayor's call.

The mayor seems to have overlooked the fact that because the townsfolk have grown up with giants in the land, they have not traveled the wide world much, Thomas realized. Those who *did* venture forth had enjoyed the company of giants when they traveled. The result was that even the captain and his guard avoided travel in the northern wilderness.

It would be hard enough, Thomas knew, to find those willing to travel south and west without giant companions. These routes had well-worn roads that led to familiar towns, mines, and quarries. But to the north? Everyone knew there were no settlements, only wild lands and danger.

As the silence lengthened, Thomas looked at Rachael. He knew his eyes betrayed the burden he felt, and he saw her eyes well up with tears. She looked into his eyes, slid her arm around his waist, and quietly mouthed the words, "Please, you don't have to be the one."

Awkward moments passed for the mayor and the crowd. Thomas squeezed Rachael's hand as tears streamed down her cheeks. Yet he felt in his heart it had to be him, and he knew Rachael felt the same. Their shared experience had taught them that such feelings were messages from above confirming the rightness of the path ahead even though they could not see it clearly.

Still, he hesitated. Rachael looked at him with pleading eyes. "The task will be difficult and full of danger," she whispered.

Mayor Nimblebone broke the silence and—with a bit less bravado than before—called again for "hearty souls" to step forward.

The crowd remained unmoved. It seemed as if the earth and skies stilled as everyone awaited a response. Thomas could no longer ignore his feelings. His curiosity about what had happened to his friend Forestmaster and the impression that he must do something grew stronger.

Thomas slowly raised his hand. The crowd around him began to buzz. By the time his arm was fully extended, the entire crowd was ablaze with the news. The mayor uttered a sigh of relief and pointed

him out. "Thomas, of field and forest, wishes to say something. Order
. . . quiet . . . let him speak."

The crowd quieted down. Thomas felt a moment of doubt and nearly shrank from his decision. He was not comfortable being the center of attention. However, overcoming the initial shock of being singled out, he said, "I guess I could try it."

It seemed a feeble response. But he knew immediately that what he said was not as important to the crowd as his willingness to say it. They turned in collective wonder, and a mighty cheer rang out. Immediately, two others agreed to accompany Thomas as far as the top of the first hilly ridge north of town. This was not particularly brave or helpful. But Thomas appreciated even this small gesture of support. It helped him face the full implications of traveling alone in the wild lands, which now began to sink in.

As the crowd surged toward him, Thomas drew his wife and daughter close. "Why don't you go on ahead? I'll be along presently. There is much to do, and I must be on my way before the shadows grow long."

Rachael nodded and squeezed his waist in a gesture of support. Then she and Hope disappeared into the crowd.

The excited crowd pushed Thomas toward the raised platform. The mayor, with great flourish, reached down and took him by the hand, pulling Thomas up next to him. Placing his hand on Thomas' shoulder, he spoke to the crowd. "Let's have another hurrah for our brave adventurer!"

"Hurrah!" the townsfolk shouted together.

Smiling broadly, the mayor pushed Thomas forward. "This may be a long and dangerous journey. Let us all do what we can to help this brave young man on his way."

The meeting ended with glad handshakes and hearty backslaps. There were offers of food from the baker, a second pair of sturdy traveling boots from his friend the shoemaker, and even a horse from the fortress stables by the captain of the guard. Thomas thanked all the well-wishers. He turned down only the offer of the horse because he had never learned to ride.

Thomas walked home surrounded by an atmosphere of celebration. But he remained untouched by it and felt increasingly alone, even as the rope maker pushed his way through the crowd to present Thomas with a coil of finely wound rope. The giantess Threadweaver, Forestmaster's wife, had taught the rope maker to produce rope that was light and unusually strong, and he was known throughout the land for his skill in rope making. Thomas accepted the gift gladly. He knew a good, strong rope in the wilderness could be as valuable as a bow or hunting knife.

The crowd thinned as Thomas approached his cottage. He was left walking only with the shoemaker. "What do you have here, my friend?" asked Thomas more cheerfully than he felt. He was deep in thought.

The shoemaker had hurried ahead to his shop and returned with the promised footwear. "These boots will serve you well and perhaps save your life one day," he replied. "They are of the sturdiest materials, and their stiffness will be of great use should you face steep passages."

Thomas thanked his friend.

When they reached the front gate, the shoemaker said, "You will be in my deepest thoughts and prayers. You must succeed, for failure would doom us all." His voice trailed off as he added, "Please, bring them back . . ."

Thomas knew the shoemaker meant well, but as he walked to his front door, the heavy weight of responsibility began to settle on his shoulders. It pressed downward, and each footstep became more difficult. He labored as if he were still carrying the elk he had claimed on a recent hunt. He thought of backing away from this journey, but then his father's words from their last walk out to the fields on that tragic day came to mind.

"Thomas," his father had said, "even in a town where little ever changes, life tends to turn in unexpected ways. I believe God intends life to happen this way. It is the best way we can become something more than we were before. It is in 'becoming something more' that we please God. Such growth furthers his purpose and enables us to find peace and true happiness in life."

"Are such moments always difficult, Father?" Thomas had asked.

"Yes, my son, but so it must be or the 'becoming' cannot take place. But you are never alone in these moments. God is always there."

This must be one of those moments Father tried to prepare me for, Thomas thought. He placed his hand on the front door's metal latch and wondered if he was equal to the task.

Thomas swung the cottage door open and immediately understood that saying goodbye to Rachael and Hope would be the hardest part. Rachael ran to his arms and said, "My dear, brave husband, why must it be you?"

He struggled to find words to comfort her, but his only response was, "Because I am here, and there is nobody else."

She spoke now with tears streaming down her cheeks. "I understand you must do this, for I feel it in my heart, as well. But I fear what could happen to you alone in the wild lands. Is not venturing out alone asking too much?"

His heart was near breaking, for there was truth in her words. Yet, he was committed and knew he must do the best he could. "What lies ahead I cannot see," he told her. "It may be good or bad, and I suspect probably some of both. But I must try, and in that trying I must give my best."

Rachel leaned her head against him. "Then I will pray that your best will be enough, my dear."

Thomas looked around for some way to calm their feelings. Hope was sitting on a stool near the fire. He took Rachael by the hand and together they sat on the floor at their daughter's feet. This settled his feelings. He explained to Hope the responsibility he had accepted and his personal curiosity about what had happened to the giants.

Hope was young. She knew only that her father was leaving on a long trip. She turned her head into his shoulder and sobbed, "I will bring you a flower every day."

"That will give me a happy thought to hold on to each day, my sweetheart. Thank you."

Hope looked up at him and smiled. "I believe in you, Daddy."

"So do I," Rachael whispered in his ear.

Thomas felt a resurgence of energy and hugged Hope and Rachael. When the warmth of the moment had sunk deep into their souls, Thomas spoke again. "Your mother and I named you Hope for a reason, my sweetheart. Do you know why?"

Hope shook her head.

"You are so named that we might remember that no matter how dark the night seems, the sun always returns to chase away the shadows."

"What are the shadows made of, Daddy?" she asked, looking a tiny bit afraid.

"Shadows are often made of fear and ignorance. Godly hope chases those shadows away. This can be a powerful force in our lives when we know there is one who always watches over us, giving us reason to have such hope."

The two-year-old seemed to understand. She nestled into her father's arms one last time and said, "I will have godly hope for you then."

"She will grow to appreciate the full meaning of your words," Rachael said. "We will talk of them often in the coming days. When you return, she will see that such hope can make a real difference and is not wasted. Even though I fear for you on your trip, good comes from it already. Understanding the power of hope will lead to faith. It enables men and women to endure and overcome. This is one of the most important gifts we can give our child."

Thomas stood facing the mantel. Above it hung the great yew bow, its quiver of carefully crafted arrows, and his hunting knife. Thomas was an expert bowman; his right index and middle fingers bore the marks of long practice. His family had enjoyed hearty dinners on many a cold night because of his skilled eye and instincts. The bowstring had to be replaced at regular intervals, but the bow itself—made of unblemished yew wood—remained as powerful, he imagined, as it had been when first made.

The bow, his father had told him, had been cut from the middle wood of a yew tree. Its wood was taken halfway between the outer sapwood and inner heartwood. This gave the bow the qualities of both woods; flexibility and strength. Thomas loved a good hunt. He knew his skill with the bow was unmatched in the village, and he never returned empty-handed.

Below the bow and its ever-present quiver hung the hunting knife. It was his favorite. Longer than a typical knife—almost two hands in length—it fit neatly in its leather scabbard on his belt. Its wide blade was of unusually fine workmanship. Who had made such a knife was a mystery to the both Thomas and the local blacksmith. He had tried unsuccessfully for years to match its hardened edge. Thomas had found endless uses for his knife in the fields and forests. Just last night he had used it to neatly slice venison into long strips to be smoked, salted, and dried for the coming winter.

Thomas took the hunting knife and scabbard from its place of honor and slipped it onto his rough leather belt. He then tied the bow and quiver to his rucksack, making sure he had a few extra bowstrings to last him on his journey.

It was time to go. Rachael helped Thomas finish packing his ruck-sack. There were tearful hugs and loving words of encouragement. He could barely mask a rising tide of anxiety.

"Please be careful and wise," Rachael pleaded with him. "Hope and I will walk to the northern ridge each day. We'll leave a wildflower as an offering for your safety and as a first sign of welcome upon your return."

Hope wrapped her arms around his leg and promised to watch for him each day.

Thomas looked into Rachael's deep brown eyes one last time and said, "Thank you for all you are and all I have become because of you."

His mind wandered. He remembered that it had been her eyes that first caught his attention when he saw her fetching water at the local well years before. They held a peace and contentment that uplifted all who were caught in her gaze. Thomas was not the only young man who had noticed her. But from that moment on he'd decided she was the one for him.

Rachael's father was the village miller. Thomas had gone out of his way to make sure he was among those assigned to deliver grain to the miller from that day forward. His father and mother had many a good laugh as they reviewed Thomas' growing list of excuses to visit the miller's home.

From their first encounters Rachael had thought him handsome, and Thomas knew she'd looked forward to his visits. However, it had taken time for her to appreciate that underneath the exterior of this rough field hand lay a truly caring and devoted gentleman. Their mar-riage had been a simple but joyous event for both families. During the following year, Thomas and Forestmaster had built the young couple's cottage.

Thomas smiled at the memory and then returned to the present. He was concerned about traveling in the wilderness alone, but he had ample clothing, food and drink, his hunting knife, bow, rope and an extra pair of good boots, courtesy of his friend the shoemaker. There was nothing more to prepare. And so, as the shadows lengthened, the young man bade farewell to the warmth of the hearth he loved most and set his face to the journey ahead.

As Thomas stepped from the front door of his cottage a shadow passed quickly through the woods far to the north west. Aiden felt he was not quite unconscious but not awake either. He fought the dense fog in his brain unsuccessfully. He could hear and feel some things but for some reason could not wake up. He knew he was being carried by a huge pair of heavily calloused hands. His clothes were soaked through and he was bouncing as if whoever or whatever cradled him was moving at a near run. Aiden tried to say something. Questions burned within him. But he could not overpower his mist filled prison.

He recalled one winter falling through the ice into a lake near his village. He was under the ice and could see people on the surface but could not reach them. He was saved by a quick thinking woodsman who used an ax to chop a hole and pull him up by the collar. There was no one to save him this time. He slipped back below the surface of his muddled consciousness and knew no more.

The Wild Lands

THOMAS BEGAN HIS journey by following the broad path left by the giants. His heart pounded the rhythm of his gait. The streets were empty. The approaching evening had given rise to new fears, and the townsfolk huddled in their homes. Not a soul stood by to wish him Godspeed. Even the two not-so-brave young men who had volunteered to walk with him to the northern ridge did not appear.

Rachael and Hope continued with him to the bottom of the northern ridge. They walked hand in hand without speaking, for there was nothing more to say. Thomas knew Rachael had a difficult path ahead and that she was terribly worried. So was he. But such feelings had already been expressed. It was time to gird oneself to the task.

Arriving at the base of the hill, Rachael turned and embraced Thomas one last time. Then she knelt down, plucked a white wildflower from the ground, and tucked it into his shirt pocket. "I miss you already," she said. "Do what you must, learn what you can, but return to me as I see you now."

"How can I not succeed, with your faith and prayers to inspire and protect me?" Thomas said, attempting to be braver than he felt. He reached down, lifted Hope in the air, and spun her around.

"Find the giants and come home soon, Daddy," she said.

He kissed her cheek. "I will do my best to find the giants. But I promise you I will return, my sweetheart." The family embraced in a three-way, lingering hug. He then turned toward his purpose and continued up to the crest of the ridge alone. With a final look back and a loving wave at Rachael and Hope, Thomas turned toward the north.

He first faced a series of hilly ridges with small valleys between each hill. A stream flowed through each valley to the east, ultimately, he supposed, to merge with the great river. He felt concern about the journey ahead but was much relieved to be on his way and doing something that could make a difference.

The atmosphere of panic in the town had been stifling, and his spirits rose as he walked in the wide world. He worried about Rachael and Hope. He had left them on their own to manage the fields, cottage, and their fears. Rachael would look out for the welfare of their friends and neighbors, as well.

Thomas moved quickly, driven by the responsibility he bore for the entire town. As he crested each hill, the view revealed nothing but more of the same. He realized his journey would be a long one. The trail he was following continued over distant ridges as far as he could see.

On the evening of the first day, he came to a large valley between two higher ridges. A sizable stream ran through the middle of the valley. Here he found the remains of what appeared to be the giants' recently abandoned long-term camp. It filled nearly the entire length of the valley. He saw where there had once been tents, cooking fires, and gathering places.

Now it was empty. Only trodden paths and well-used cooking areas remained. He knew the giant people loved the land, but he was amazed that they could live in a location such as this for so long and leave it uncluttered. The valley would soon completely recover, its natural vegetation erasing all evidence of the giants' camp. He was pleased that he had learned something on his journey already. The giants had lived among them for a long time, but they had been staying here in temporary structures each night.

This means the giants knew all along that their time with the people of my village was limited, Thomas concluded. "Why was this never spoken of?" he asked aloud. "How could such a great secret be kept for so long?"

The valley remained mute, revealing none of her secrets. Thomas knew he must continue on to find the answers. He stayed the night in the giants' temporary camp. He wondered what it must have been like during the evenings when the giants gathered for meals and fellowship. He would have loved to have sat around a campfire just once, listening to the hopes, joys, thoughts, and general discussion of giants. *I could have learned so much!*

The next day, Thomas continued to follow the trail over ridges and valleys. Each valley became smaller than the last. Each stream grew shallower. Later that day, he crossed mostly dry stream beds waiting for the rainy season. He was careful to fill his containers with water whenever he could.

By the third day of his journey through the rolling hills, he was glad he had done so. The streams he was crossing were completely dry.

He crested the last ridge at midday and was troubled by what he saw. A broad, dry plain, flat as a tabletop, spread out before him. Nothing taller than sagebrush grew there, and he could see no water or shade. Thomas brought down a sage grouse with one of his arrows. The bird was a welcome change of diet from his smoked, salted meats. Eating the fresh game raised his spirits, although the dryness of the land remained a concern.

Thomas could not continue long without water, so he began limiting his intake to make it last as long as possible. After two days crossing the plain, his last flask of water ran low, then entirely dry. With an empty flask and no streams to replenish it, Thomas knew that if he didn't find water soon he would be in real trouble.

A third day passed with no relief. He was feeling the effects of exhaustion from a lack of water and the dry heat. The ground consisted of fine, powdery dirt, and the few plants that grew here were of the hearty, deep-rooted variety that rarely saw moisture.

At one point during the day his heart leaped. Thomas could have sworn he saw water shimmering just ahead. But as he ran forward, the image disappeared like a ghostly lake, taunting his thirst. He had heard the traders talk about "fools' watering holes." Tales were told of travelers gone mad running from one vanishing phantom to the next. They'd lost their minds in the belief that if they could just get to the next one before it vanished, they would be able to drink. These visions are merely tricks of nature, Thomas realized. He ignored them and stayed steady on his course.

Near the end of the third day, he was seriously dehydrated and could barely walk. If he had been able to muster the strength to turn back, he would have done so. But it was too late. Water was too far behind to save him. His only hope lay in continuing to move forward. Thomas was tempted to drop his pack. It felt so heavy! But that would be giving up, and he was determined to fight to the end.

Thomas knew he might not make it through another day. *But if it ends here in this flat, arid plain,* he thought, *then it will be while doing what I promised to do.* He kept going only because he mumbled over and over his promise to the townsfolk: "I guess I could try."

He stumbled and fell at the end of the day, sending a cloud of fine dust into the air. It settled on his motionless form, for there was not the slightest hint of a breeze. Thomas lay there without the strength to spread out his bedroll or set a fire. He had dropped his rucksack in the dirt and now crawled to lay his head on the roll.

Thomas reached a hand into his pack and pulled out a piece of salted meat. "I must try to eat something to preserve my strength," he said in a weak voice. But his cracked lips stung from the meat's saltiness. As swollen as his mouth, tongue, and throat were, it was impossible to swallow anything, anyway. He rolled onto his back, let the meat fall into the dust, and immediately lost consciousness.

A few hours later, a large, black emperor scorpion wandered by, foraging in the moonlight. It inspected Thomas' hand and crawled over his fingers. The scorpion then moved to the salted meat. Finding it more to its liking, it dragged the prize to its den. Thomas didn't stir.

As Thomas' exhausted mind sought unsuccessfully for rest, he found himself standing on the edge of his fields back home. He could see newly plowed rows and his father standing far out into the fields, calling him to come closer. Thomas obeyed, but as he approached the spot where his father stood, he found nothing but the rich, loamy furrows. He looked around anxiously. There were no footsteps to follow.

Desperate for a clue, he looked up and saw his father again, standing at the far side of the fields. He stood near the spot where Thomas and Forestmaster had been working together that last day. His father beckoned to Thomas again, more earnestly this time.

Thomas hesitated. He remembered the vanishing images of water and wondered if the vision of his father was another trick of nature or if this was what it was like to go mad. He rubbed his eyes. His father was still there, motioning urgently. Thomas ran this time, into his father's outstretched arms. They enfolded each other in a warm embrace.

Thomas choked out the words, "I miss you, father." He looked around. They were standing in the location where six months ago his father had been pinned under the fallen tree that ended his life.

As he stood wrapped in his father's arms, Thomas heard him say, "You have done well, my son . . . do not doubt . . . you have strength yet to continue. Do not give up! I believe in you."

Thomas cried dry tears, for he had no moisture to wet his eyes. "How can I?" he said. "I have nothing left to give to this journey. I am spent and will surely perish by midday tomorrow. I have failed, Father." Overwhelmed by fatigue and grief, Thomas fell to his knees.

His father knelt beside him and took his hand. "My son, I have walked with you hand in hand your whole life. Do not think death prevents me from doing so now. Stand with me and take my hand. We will walk together one more day."

Thomas looked into his father's eyes and said, "I guess I could try for one more day."

The dream evaporated as suddenly as it had come. Thomas opened his eyes to discover the sun beginning to peek over the eastern horizon. "Yes Father," he mumbled, "I guess I could try for one more day."

Thomas held out his hand and felt something, yet saw nothing. He stood shakily, shouldered his pack, and began to walk. Several steps later, he stumbled. He caught himself and took several more steps before another near collapse. Each step became more successful than the last, until he was walking slowly but steadily toward the north, following the giant's trail again.

Morning turned to early afternoon and still there was no change. Thomas didn't know how much longer he could continue, but he kept repeating the words, "Yes, Father, I guess I could try for one more day," and "Please don't let go." He was amazed to realize that he was still moving forward as the shadows lengthened that fourth day.

He began to perceive a dark line in the distance. It ran across the entire horizon ahead. *Is this another trick of nature?* he wondered. As he continued, he noticed it was not moving, not like the shimmering images before. He began to hope. "This is something different," he said, "and anything different has to be better."

The shadow was still far ahead—right at the edge of his vision—but it slowly grew. As the day waned, Thomas recognized it as a towering forest. He quickened his pace. *Where there are great trees there must be water!* he reasoned. He reached the trees as the sun was touching the western mountains and discovered a small stream running just inside the forest's edge.

Thomas collapsed face first into the stream. He drank in long, cool draughts of the delicious, clear water. Then he rolled over and rested in the stream, gazing at the sky and feeling the water trickle over his spent body. He felt humbled by the gift of such a dream and the memories of his father. They had walked hand in hand one more time, and they had made it. He lay in the stream and cried his gratitude.

Thomas saw the hand of a loving God in his life-saving dream. He hoped his Maker and his father both knew how he felt. He mentally listed all the blessings he had received throughout his life. But he particularly hoped they were aware of his appreciation of those gifts that had saved him during the day just ended.

Thomas filled his flasks and made camp for the evening, glad to leave the plains behind. He heard wild-sounding animal voices during the night. Most were comforting sounds, except for the occasional howl of a wolf. Wolves could be a real danger, Thomas thought. But these sounded far away, and he rested without concern.

Aiden felt himself climbing toward consciousness again. He was aware of his senses but still could not speak, move or open his eyes. It was as if heavy weights held them down. *I am in a room now,* he thought. The bed was soft as were the voices. He heard one say, "I don't know how long it will take or if there will ever be a change."

Another voice answered, "Isn't there anything more you can do?"

The first voice spoke again, "He has a good poultice in him and is breathing calmly, the rest is up to his will and that of Worldmaker."

"I am here! I am alive! Can't you hear me?" Aiden yelled in his mind. But there was no sound. He felt it happening again. He was sinking back into the dark depths.

Aiden heard the second speaker's voice fade as they apparently exited the room, "It is such a tragedy. I was so close, if I could only have reached him sooner."

The Sea of Fallen Trees

THE NEXT MORNING, Thomas entered the forest. The trees were sparse initially, allowing easy passage. Over the course of the day, however, the forest thickened—not only with trees but also with undergrowth that made it increasingly difficult to get through. Thomas was still regaining the strength he had lost over the previous days on the dry plain so he stopped frequently to rest.

On several occasions, Thomas needed his hunting knife to slash through the thick brush. He had not lost the giants' broad path; it was still there. But he discovered that giants could step over many obstacles with little notice. However, following such a path was a very different matter for a man on foot.

Each successive stream he crossed became larger until he arrived at a wide river that required him to search for a safe place to cross. The river was deep and ran swiftly, and Thomas could not swim.

To find a safe crossing, Thomas had to travel half a day's journey out of his way. He finally came to a ford that looked shallow enough to try. Thomas moved slowly across the fast-moving river. He could feel watery fingers tugging at his legs, trying to drag him down. The round slippery river stones shifted under each step, making it hard to keep his balance. The icy water came up only to his knees, but one careless moment—a slip on a loose stone—and the current would sweep him away, drowning him for sure.

His heart pounded in his chest. Sweat formed in beads on his forehead as he carefully moved his feet from one unsure foothold to another. He slipped to his knees once and steadied himself on all fours before moving again. Thomas wished he had spent less time in the forest climbing trees as a lad and more time at the bridge over the eastern river learning to swim. This was not a crossing for a farmer like Thomas, who could barely keep his head above water.

But on this day there was no other way but through the river. *I must finish what I started.* He kept his legs widely spaced against the current and finally made it to the northern bank. He sat down and looked back; amazed that he had made it across. His breathing was rapid and shallow. However, he needed only a short rest. Then Thomas picked up his pace, glad to be moving on solid ground again.

During the afternoon of his journey's tenth day, he came to the edge of a deep blue lake. At first it appeared that the trail ended at the lake's edge. Through the clear water, however, Thomas saw deep giant footprints in the bottom silt. The giants had walked or swum right through the middle of the lake! The trail showed no sign of hesitation or milling around on the bank. It just continued into the lake as if it were a small, inconvenient puddle.

Thomas sat down on the rocky beach. "Now what?" he asked aloud. "I have passed over hill and valley, plain and forest, thicket and river, and for what? To be drowned in a lake?" He was worn down and made camp along the shore. He put off his decision on how to proceed. Perhaps his mind would be clearer in the morning.

That night, for the first time, the howling wolves concerned him. There seemed to be many, moving in groups or packs. Wolves were usually night hunters and vicious enough by themselves. But in a pack, they were intelligent and deadly to beast or man. Thomas made a large fire and slept as close to it as the heat and flame would allow.

The morning dawned crisp and cool. Thomas constructed a spear by lashing an arrow to a straight ash tree limb. He then tied a length of rope to the makeshift spear so he could retrieve it after each throw. Many nice-sized trout swam in the shallows, and it didn't take long to spear one and enjoy breakfast.

A full belly and a good night's sleep made all the difference. Thomas began to search for the best way to proceed. He noticed the lake's eastern bank was mostly clear of brush. He determined to follow the edge of the lake around until he came to where the giant's trail emerged from the other side. This worked well but took most of the day. As evening fell, Thomas arrived at the place where the path resumed. However, what he found there dismayed him almost to the point of declaring defeat.

This may prove to be the most difficult part of my journey, Thomas thought with a heavy heart. Before him lay an immense forest denser than any he had experienced. Huge trees had fallen or been knocked aside—apparently by the giants to clear a passage—and lay scattered on the ground. It was nothing for a giant to step over these trees, but it created a great maze of trunks, branches, and greenery for Thomas. Many downed trees had trunks as thick as a man is tall. Thomas could walk around some of them, but more often he needed to climb over. Each climb required his rope and steps carved in the trunks to gain a foothold.

Great holes where the uprooted trees had stood presented additional difficulties. Some holes were as large as his cottage with a depth twice his height. His progress slowed to a crawl. Two weeks had passed since he'd waved goodbye to Rachael and Hope. He was no closer, it seemed, to finding the answers he sought.

Each night, Thomas heard the wolves howling and hunting. Though he always built and remained near a large fire, the wolves seemed to be overcoming their fear and moving closer. Luminous eyes watched from the shadows. He occasionally caught glimpses of great, grey, furry coats on the edge of his lit campsite. The prints he found each morning revealed that these beasts were large. Their howls sounded wanton and hungry. How long would it take before they overcame their fear and attacked?

After several days of calm weather, the skies turned dark. Rain fell in sheets that turned the forest of fallen timber into a nightmare of crumbling bark and calf-deep, oozing mud. Thomas continued, but his pace slowed as each fallen tree he climbed over became a slippery mess. He was working his way over yet another in what seemed an endless succession of large trunks when it happened.

The howling began again. It was nearer than ever, yet their grey forms stayed hidden by the heavy rainfall. He felt that any moment could end with a huge beast leaping out of the gray, drenching veil. Thomas quickened his pace. While working his way over a particularly rotten trunk, the wet bark gave way. He tumbled down the far side of the trunk into one of the great, deep tree holes.

Thomas lay still, mentally checking his body to be sure nothing was broken. He winced from a large bruise on his left shoulder. He must have hit a branch or the curve of the trunk as he fell. Rising painfully onto his good shoulder, then to his feet, he looked around and realized he was in grave danger.

The walls of the hole were soft and muddy from the rain, making climbing out impossible. A wide stream of rainwater was rushing into the hole, filling it rapidly. Treading water as the hole filled was not an option—it would soon wear him out. He looked around for anything he might use to escape. There was nothing. The water was up to his knees and rising. He had little time. With each passing minute, the hole looked more and more like a murky grave. Thomas mumbled a quick but sincere prayer for help.

Suddenly, he remembered his bow and the rope. It had worked for spear fishing; perhaps he could try the same idea here. As the water reached his waist, he tied the rope to the end of an arrow and nocked it in his bow. The other end of the rope he tied around his waist. Trunks rose up on both sides of the hole. He aimed and released the arrow with a prayer that it would sink deeply into one of the trunks and hold fast long enough for him to escape.

Thomas yanked on the rope. It went slack, and his heart sank. As fast as he could, he pulled the arrow back and recoiled the rope for another shot. He let loose a second time and pulled hard on the rope. It went slack again, *Is there time for another try?* he thought and quickly pulled the rope in.

With muddy water oozing like melted chocolate up to his chest, Thomas knew he might not have time for another shot. As he drew in the rope, it suddenly jerked tight and held fast. What it had caught on was unimportant. Without a second thought, he pulled himself up out of the hole, slipping and banging against the side. Just as the water reached the height of a man—and would have sealed his muddy fate— he flopped over the edge and onto the pine-covered ground.

Thomas collapsed on his back, grateful for his miraculous escape. He lay there for some time, looking up at the storm clouds and feeling the rain on his filthy face and clothes. Slowly, he regained his strength.

I have to find a place to set a fire and dry out before continuing my journey. Thomas slogged through the thick ooze, following the rope to see where the arrow had lodged. To his surprise, the arrow had not stuck anywhere. It lay loose on the ground. In wonderment and gratitude, he thanked God for his good fortune and continued on his wet, muddy way.

The heavy rain fell for most of the night, making it difficult for Thomas to keep his campfire going. It was impossible to dry his clothing, but the rain beating down on him did serve to wash away much of the mud. At some point during the night, the rain ceased. Morning dawned wet but bright and clear.

Thomas relit his fire and hung his clothes and bedroll on branches near the fire to dry. Then he rested. Only then was he able to repack his rucksack and continue his journey. He was pleased to see he had reached the end of the sea of fallen trees. His spirits lifted and his pace quickened.

He still walked in the forest, but it had noticeably thinned. The land rose toward the great northern mountains.

Each evening, he had kept a strong fire to ward off the beasts he heard howling and hunting just out of sight. He felt his loneliness most in the evenings. It was enough some nights to nearly cause him to turn for home.

This was one of those nights.

An Unexpected Guest

THE FOREST WAS full of wildlife. Thomas had managed to bring down two squirrels with well-placed arrows. They were dressed and roasting on sticks over the fire. The clearing he had chosen was wide, with dense underbrush on the northern and western edges.

The roasting meat was ready to eat when he heard rustling in the bushes near the northern edge of the clearing. The sound was that of something bigger than a squirrel and less stealthy than a deer. He retrieved his bow, nocked an arrow, and sat near the fire until late in the evening, watching and waiting.

He ate the meat of one of the squirrels and pronounced it a "fine meal," as if to torment the hunting wolf pack. As the fire burned low and darkness closed in, the fog that comes before sleep began to slip into Thomas' mind. He was nodding off, but through the creeping numbness of sleep he thought he heard something unusual. He came fully alert and listened intently to be sure it was not just a waking dream.

The noise came again, faint but nevertheless there. He listened with all his senses alert as the rustling seemed to take on human quali-ties. Just as this thought dawned on him, the sounds of the forest went suddenly and completely silent. Then the bushes rustled again. An aged and withered wraith of a man appeared at the edge of the clearing.

Thomas rose quickly, drew his bow, and stood still, awaiting the next move. He'd heard stories of robbers in the wilderness who often used trickery to gain the confidence of their prey, so as to catch them off guard.

Holding up his hands as if he could ward off a flying arrow with mere flesh, the ancient figure spoke. "Please allow an old traveler a seat and perhaps some drink and food." Struggling to gain another breath, he continued, "I have wandered far without sustenance or human companionship and have need of both this evening."

Wary and watchful, Thomas said, "You are welcome to sit and take meat at my fire, old man, but I am wary of the dangers in these lands and will continue my vigilance as we speak."

The old man shuffled toward the fire, leaning heavily on an old staff he used like a cane. He shook his head in understanding—or perhaps simply as a result of some advanced disease or palsy. "Watch all you wish. I shall not feel any safer than I already am."

Though it was clear the old man was nearly starving, his eating was slow and deliberate. All the while he watched Thomas intently. The old man was covered almost completely with an ankle-length, dirty, brown robe—if that was what it could still be called. It was moth-eaten and tattered nearly to ruin.

His hands bore long thin fingers covered with skin that seemed to be stretched tightly across the bones. The man's overgrown, pointed fingernails made his hands appear more like the talons of some great eagle than a human. Thomas felt less threatened as time went on. However, with the forest continuing its ghostly silence, he remained uncomfortable.

The old man continued eating and finished the squirrel without speaking. Then he licked his fingers, smacked his thin lips, and leaned back. "What finds you alone in these wilds at night, my generous friend?" he asked.

Thomas did not answer but continued to scan the surrounding woods.

"Please, take a seat. You are safe here this evening," the old man assured him.

Thomas eased his stance and said, "I seek the giants who have worked alongside us as friends my whole life and the life of my father and his father before him. Without warning, the giants disappeared, leaving only a great, wide highway of footprints trailing to the north." As he spoke, Thomas settled onto a fallen tree near the fire.

"You seek more than you know, my young friend," the old man said. Compassion touched his voice. "Yet you travel alone. Are you a great warrior or ambassador of your people?"

Thomas chuckled. "I am one who is like any other from my simple village. I am alone because no one dared walk at my side in the wild world."

"Ah," the old man said almost to himself. "Yes, there must be One in each village." A smile curled his lip.

"One in each village?"

"Yes, One who knows," replied the visitor.

"Knows what?" Thomas asked in frustration. He did not have patience for riddles.

"One who has answered the question for his people," the old man replied, as if every living thing in the forest knew of what he spoke and no further explanation was necessary.

I wander in the wilds risking my life for many long days. And my first human interaction is with a crazy old man. Realizing he would get little from this current conversation, Thomas decided to try a different approach. "Do you know where the giants have gone? Is it worth trying to follow?"

"Ah, yes. It is worth every difficult step you take to follow the path that life has placed you on, my young fellow." He looked northward into the dark for several seconds. Thomas saw that the old man had bright, intelligent eyes, something he had not noticed before.

The old man broke his apparent trance and said, as if he had made an important decision, "It is far but not too far. Do not falter now. There is a great barrier, but there is always a way." Speaking as if out of breath, he continued, "I must leave . . . thank you for your hospitality . . . you will not regret any kindness shown this night." With those words he rose, shuffled toward the edge of the light and disappeared into the woods.

Thomas was stunned by the abruptness of the old man's departure. *He eats my food and gives me riddles in answer to my questions then leaves as suddenly as he arrived.* He was wondering at the strange encounter when he turned back to the fire and noticed the old man's gnarled walking staff. It had been left leaning against the stump on which he sat.

"Hey!" he called out to the darkness, "Hey, old man, you forgot your . . ." His sentence went unfinished, for the forest suddenly came alive with sounds. He called out again, but there was no response from the old man.

Thomas tied the walking stick to the side of his rucksack. *Surely,* he thought, *the old man will realize his mistake and return.* Feeling more exhausted than he ever remembered, he threw a few logs on the fire to keep it burning brightly and then quickly laid out his bedroll. He pondered the strange encounter as he gazed at the stars set in the black-draped night sky. Thomas drifted deeply into a well-deserved sleep.

He never imagined that a large shadow watched him quietly from the edge of the clearing.

The Great Barrier

THE NEXT MORNING dawned bright and clear. Thomas rose early with renewed energy for his quest. He could tell he was beginning the long ascent toward the northern mountains now visible in the distance. The trail became steeper, and each evening the air grew cooler. He found the gnarled walking stick useful as he labored up the ever-steepening path.

On his third day's journey from the camp where he'd met the old man, Thomas reached the foot of a sheer wall of rock. The great, wide trail vanished. He searched all day for a way around the barrier, but was unsuccessful. Thomas finally decided that the only way the giants could have gone was directly over the top.

How can I hope to go this way? Thomas wondered. It appeared to be a nearly smooth granite face. *But I must make the attempt.* Fatigued from a long day's travel, and with the sun setting, he decided to wait until morning.

He searched the foot of the mountain face for a good place to bed down and set a fire. There was something strangely uncomfortable about the area. *Bones.* Bones were everywhere, bones of all sizes and kinds scattered on the ground. Thomas could scarcely walk without stepping on one. They appeared to be animal bones but he couldn't be sure. Coming upon them made him feel dark and hopeless, and he wished he could move on immediately. He dealt with his feeling of dread by setting up camp some distance back down the trail. He had to get away from this unpleasant location.

Thomas built a strong fire, roasted and ate a rabbit he had collected and cleaned earlier in the day, and collapsed into his bedroll. The next day would require skills he had never practiced before except when climbing trees as a lad. *The great mountain before me will be nothing like climbing a tree,* he mused.

Like every night, the howling and rustling of the wolves disturbed his dreams. *I am sure they are watching.* In frustration, he called out to the night, "Why don't you just do it? Attack me now and get it over with or leave me alone." Thomas was tired of being the rodent in this game of cat and mouse. The wolves' lurking in the bushes just out of sight made him feel like wounded prey. It was as if they were waiting until he was weak enough to take him without a fight.

As Thomas drifted into a fitful sleep he wondered if it would be easier to find his way up the mountain in the daylight. Then his mind wandered to darker thoughts. *Will I awake staring into the faces of a dozen starving beasts? Or will tomorrow to be the day I do not wake up at all?*

He did wake up, and it was to a beautiful sunrise. Thomas felt grateful and happy to bid good morning to such a day. However, he was still troubled by the lack of identifiable paths up the mountain. Nevertheless, he decided the time had come.

Thomas felt he would either succeed or fail in his journey before the sun set. He packed his rucksack tightly and prepared to attempt the climb. He decided this was the ideal time to use the stiff new pair of boots the shoemaker had given him, so he slipped them on. They felt solid and snug on his feet and would serve him well during the ascent. Thomas continued his preparations for the day uninterrupted.

As he was sliding the walking stick into the side of his rucksack, he heard the ever-present howling of the wolves suddenly grow louder and closer. There were more of them now, and he sensed a change in their howls, as if a deadly plan were in motion. He quickly shouldered his pack and headed toward the rock face.

Thomas heard the rustling in the bushes grow nearer. He broke into a desperate run, sensing it had become a race for his life. Blood-thirsty howls came from every direction. It dawned on him what the wolves' plan was and why there were so many bones strewn at the base of the mountain. They had trailed him to the dead end at the rock face. There they would work as a pack to encircle and claim their prey.

The piles of bones told Thomas that he was not the first to fool-ishly make a stand against such odds in this deadly place. He knew he could take down a couple of the powerful beasts with his bow and per-haps another with his hunting knife. But stopping to do so was a fool's errand, for their numbers would quickly overwhelm him.

He ran now with all his strength. As the wall became visible through the woods he noticed a series of rough-hewn niches in the rock face. *How did I miss these when I searched the face last night?* he thought. *These niches just might be the answer.* Yet as he approached the steps, he feared his climb would not be fast enough. The wolves were too close.

Thoughts of Rachael and Hope flashed through his mind and gave him an extra burst of speed. It was now a simple calculation of speed and distance. His keen senses and mind performed it instantly and told him the wolves would win.

Thomas pushed himself harder. His legs felt like rubber after mak-ing the uphill run with a full pack. He consigned himself to his fate and prepared to turn and face his doom. He reached for his knife, felt its handle in his hand. Yes, he would turn . . . *now*!

Suddenly, a large, jagged boulder hit the ground with a crashing boom, shaking the earth ten feet behind him. The boulder landed on the nearest wolf just as it gathered its powerful body for a final deadly leap.

The crash startled the wolves. They paused and withdrew several paces. They seemed to be reconsidering their prey. Was this some unexpected new threat or simply a coincidence of nature?

Thomas sensed the boulder had only given him a few moments. He had one chance to do this right. He whirled and made for the niches. His motion caused the closest wolves to renew their pursuit, followed immediately by the entire pack. They quickly closed the distance and prepared to strike. He could hear their rabid breathing rising to frenzied excitement. A kill was almost in their grasp!

Approaching the wall, Thomas used the first step to launch himself up to the second small step. He quickly scrambled up four more just as the first two wolves sprang. He misjudged their massive power. A pair or steel jaws clamped down on his pant leg, grazing his flesh. Thomas felt the pull of gravity and the weight of the beast nearly capture him. Then his pant leg tore, leaving a long, ragged rip. The wolf fell away and landed with a dull *thud* on the bone-strewn ground below.

Thomas continued climbing until the niches ended at what appeared to be a carved ledge just wide enough to sit on. He caught his breath and rested, while the wolves—over a dozen now—circled and howled in anger thirty feet below. A stream of blood flowed freely from his calf. Thomas was grateful for the narrow escape.

Thomas flushed his wound with water from his flask. Then he tore several strips from his already ragged pant leg and used them to wrap his leg the best he could. He was thankful for his good fortune. The wound was more a glancing blow than a deep cut. It had missed muscle and bone and should not hamper his climb.

After a brief rest, Thomas scanned the rock face to determine the safest route up. He was surprised to note that the carved niches looked more like steps. They ended at the small ledge upon which he was sitting. It was as if the steps and the ledge were intended specifically as a place of safety against such a threat.

While there were no carved niches above him, the mountain appeared to be more jagged than sheer, allowing numerous foot and hand holds. Further progress was possible, although it would be difficult, dangerous, and slow.

The small ledge upon which he now rested was no place to linger. The wolves below, robbed of a sure kill, were in frenzy, milling and jumping to reach him. Any thought of backtracking was impossible. He must continue upward.

Scrambling up cracks and along ledges all day, Thomas discovered he was only half way to the summit at nightfall. The injury to his leg was painful and beginning to swell. He cleaned and bandaged it again, but he had no herbs to treat the infection. The slice from the wolf's razor-sharp teeth was full of dirt and pus that could not be adequately cleansed with what he had on hand. He labored onward but was beginning to feel dizzy and faint.

Then the rain began to fall.

A Voice in the Dark

RAIN IN THE northern mountains, Thomas discovered, came down in drops the size of olives. When these drops hit, they soaked through every layer of clothing, right to the skin. He was drenched in less than a minute. The rain's force loosened and dislodged rocks that rumbled past him into the distance. Lightning split the air; thunder boomed instantly with each flash.

The storm—combined with the rigors of his climb and the increasing pain in his leg—wore Thomas down. He could go no further. Night closed in and the rocky path quickly became slippery. He managed to collapse into a cold spot in the cleft of a rock, where he lay for several moments. The unforgiving rain still pelted him, but at least he could rest his leg.

Thomas lifted his head and was encouraged to discover that the cleft opened into a larger crevice further in. As he crawled along the narrow way into the crevice, he was satisfied to find it was a bit wider, although still exposed to the storm. Thomas looked ahead again. To his great relief, the crevice opened into an enormous cave.

With what seemed his last measure of strength, Thomas dragged himself out of the rain and sat just inside the mouth of the cave. He was tired, but he knew he must tend to his leg first. He unwrapped the blood-soaked rags and was alarmed to find a halo of reddish skin surrounding the still-oozing injury.

Sharp pain shot up his leg each time he put weight on it. Thomas knew this was not good but he could only wash and rebind the wound with more strips from his pant leg. After doing what he could for the injury, he spread out his bedroll and prepared for a much-needed rest. It had been a terribly long and difficult day, but he felt grateful that he had made it this far.

Just then, he heard something that made him freeze.

Is something scuffling behind me in the depths of the cave? He listened intently. The scuffling came again. Most people would have easily missed the sound, Thomas realized. But the events of the past days had sharpened his senses, and they were all focused at that moment.

Then came the soft noise of something scraping along the floor of the cave. It was not a pebble or a rock loosened by seeping water and pulled from some higher place by gravity. It was not the wind. Thomas' hunting skills were now fully alert. He knew that only living things made the kind of sound he had just heard.

He soundlessly drew his hunting knife and backed against the wall of the cave, ignoring his injured leg. This position required that whatever had made the scuffling sound would have to approach him from the front. He was as ready as could be.

The space was too tight for his bow to be helpful. He half crouched and waited for whatever would come next. Thomas listened for several moments but heard no further sounds. He began to relax. "I must be hearing things or going crazy or both," he said aloud.

Suddenly, a voice boomed from the inky darkness of the cave. "Why do you disturb my slumber?" It was so loud it startled Thomas, causing him to stumble backward. He tripped and slid against the wall.

"Be gone!" the mighty voice howled.

"I have traveled far and am tired," Thomas said weakly. "Can we not share this dry cave for a few hours? Then I will leave you in peace."

"I do not seek company, nor do I care for your story. *Be . . . gone!*" growled the voice. A stone twice the size of Thomas' head flew past him and out the cave entrance. Had he not instinctively moved to the wall of the cave, the discussion would have been over. He would have been knocked off the ledge at the mouth of the cave and his bones added to those below.

Thomas knew the next few seconds were critical if he wanted to stay alive—a dry night's sleep was the least of his problems. He had to do something to change the nature of this conversation, so he hit upon a different tack. "Do you know any giants?" he asked.

There was a slight pause. His question seemed to have caught the voice off guard. "I have no use for giants," came the response.

Encouraged by the change in the voice's tone, Thomas pushed on. "Perhaps you are right. I don't know what to think about them, either. They were our friends, but they disappeared one morning without a word. I have been sent by my people to find out why."

At this there was some more scuffling and a couple of grunts. Suddenly, Thomas found himself staring into the face of the dirtiest, meanest-looking giant he had ever seen.

Even a smallish giant, which this one appeared to be, was a sight to behold. This giant, appearing so quickly out of the darkness, was the greatest shock thus far in a journey full of surprises. He was filthy and carried a stench that made Thomas want to hold his breath. The giant's hair was knotted and matted with grease. He had an unkempt beard full of food and dirt. His clothes were rags that hung loosely on his large frame. His eyes were tired and red, and the giant's face looked like it had been a very long time since he had smiled.

"You were left alone without a word?" asked the giant.

"Yes. It has been hard for my people. They are afraid and don't know what to do," Thomas said, feeling the burden of his responsibilities return.

"You are alone in the wild lands, as am I," the giant said sadly.

"I am not alone by choice," said Thomas, "but no one else would join me on my journey. You are a giant. Why are *you* alone?"

"I no longer wish to be alone," the giant said in remorse. "But there were many years when I desired to be free from my people and make my own choices with no rules to bind me." He was quiet for a moment then continued, "I refused the counsel of my elder giants. I rejected the goodness of the earth and the joy that comes from serving. I left to find myself, or so I thought. Life with the giant people seemed so limited. I believed that anything I found out in the wild world would be better."

"What did you find?" asked Thomas.

The giant's face twisted in anguish and he put his massive head in his hands. "Nothing. I have found *nothing*! I sought only for what satisfied me and saw responsibility as a burden. I have learned that such pursuits are simply selfishness disguised with different clothing. Seeking such brings only sadness, loneliness, and in the end bitterness. These things are *nothing*!"

He sobbed for several moments. Thomas dared not speak. It was clear the giant was not finished. He now spoke between sobs. "And . . . I desperately desire . . . *something* . . . of my life back."

Thomas knew this was an important moment in both their lives. He sought for something meaningful to say. Then he imagined his daughter standing with a wildflower in her hand waving to him. As if a light dawned in his mind, he knew exactly what the giant needed to hear.

"No one is ever lost, no matter how hard they try or how terrible their life has been. You may have strayed far from your path but there is always a way back. This is called 'godly hope.' You have it in you, I'm sure."

"But my people! It has been so long and I am but a shadow of what I was," said the giant. "Surely, I have become worthless in their eyes."

Thomas thought he was making progress, so he shifted the conversation again. "I am called Thomas. What are you called?"

"I was known as Horsetender and was learning to care for our many herds of beasts. I loved the animals, but there were so many things to learn. I was impatient and thought the wide world could offer something different . . . easier," answered the giant with pain in his voice.

"I have lived with giants all my life. They are forgiving and caring. Surely, they will take you back," Thomas reassured Horsetender. "I will speak with them when I come to their land, but you must have hope. Hope will lead you back to faith, which in turn will give you the power to change."

"It is a hard thing to consider," Horsetender said. He now seemed fully aware of his ragged appearance. "I am dirty and unfit in every way. They will turn me away."

Thomas almost agreed. Horsetender was neither pleasant to look at nor to smell. But because Thomas believed he knew the giants well, he said, "The giants are a good people. They will not dwell on what you have been or even on what you appear to be. Rather, they will rejoice with you in the goodness of your heart and what you will choose to become." Then he added with a hint of a smile, "But it wouldn't hurt to take a bath in the river before you return."

Horsetender laughed at this and glanced down at himself. It was perhaps the first real laugh he had laughed in a very long while. Then the giant took a good long look at Thomas. He seemed to notice the torn pant leg and injury for the first time. "But, young traveler," he said. "You are hurt and it festers."

"Yes," answered Thomas wearily. "It would have been fatal had the wolf been a step closer when he leapt."

"You are fortunate. The wolves in the woods below hunt in large packs, which are dangerous even for most giants. I have tended to horses with injuries like yours and know of a poultice that can be made of roots and herbs that will draw out the infection," the giant said. "Your words have awakened in me feelings that I have been unwilling to consider for a long time. Perhaps I can do something in return. You are tired. Sleep now, and thank you for your encouraging words. It has been a long time since I have had anyone to talk to. You may stay the night. You are not far from your goal." The giant retreated back into the darkness.

Echoing from the far reaches of the cave, his final words came back. "My nose tells me you are right about taking a bath, and my heart tells me you are also right about this 'godly hope' of which you speak. Perhaps it is time to try both."

The Top of the World

THE MORNING DAWNED cold and frosty. Thomas was as sore as he ever remembered being. He hobbled to his feet. A brief search of the cave revealed that Horsetender was gone. However, an oversized bowl sat next to his bedroll. In it was a greenish, foul-smelling mash of what looked like a variety of weeds, roots, grains, and mud. This must be the healing poultice Horsetender spoke of, Thomas guessed.

It smelled even worse than Horsetender did. Thomas hoped it was not intended to be eaten. There were no instructions, so Thomas took the less stomach-turning approach and spread it on his injury. He then tore up strips of cloth from his other pant leg and wrapped the paste tightly against his wound. The rest he kept wrapped in another strip of cloth tied and dangling from his pack. He was not stuffing that horrible, smelly substance in his rucksack with his extra clothes.

Thomas immediately felt a tingling from his wound. He hoped it meant something good was happening. "Time will tell," he told himself. There was nothing more to do but continue upward as best he could. Fortunately, he had a change of clothes, for those he was wearing were in tatters from the climb and from wrapping his leg.

The summit was in sight now. The night's rain had washed much of the loose material from his route, improving his handholds and footholds. His climb became steeper as he neared the summit. One particular overhang caused him to work far to his right to get around. The muscles and tendons in his fingers were so fatigued he could barely hold on. Finally, as afternoon was turning to evening, his hands curled over the last ledge and he heaved himself up.

He stood on the summit and looked back with satisfaction at the lands he had spent weeks traversing. The sun was riding on the horizon, giving the sky a beautiful orange glow. The world may be a wild and dangerous place, but from this majestic perch it was also immensely beautiful.

Thomas wished he could share this view with his wife and daughter. They both had a keen sense of the beauties of the world that surrounded them. He sat reverently as the sun set and shadows filled the valleys far below. He marveled at the darkening auburn sky, which stretched out to touch him here at the top of the world.

With the valleys now resting in darkness and the sun's last rays bathing the summit, Thomas moved away and found a place a safe distance from the edge to set up camp for the night. The summit was treeless, except for one stout oak. It had battled its way out of a crevice in the thick stone skin of the great mountain and stood near a deep, blue pool of water that appeared to have collected from the storm.

Tufts of moss or lichen cushioned his bedroll, but his rest could not have been called comfortable. There was no fuel for a fire so he would have to go without. Thomas checked his leg, which looked and felt better, and applied the remainder of the poultice, wrapping it tightly. He was completely spent. Within moments of lying down, he found himself drifting into his first deep sleep in two days.

No wolves howled to disturb him, and only a great, grey wood owl passed overhead during the night. It circled twice and wondered what strange visitor lay in his hunting grounds. Thomas slept a bit longer than was his custom but awoke feeling refreshed. His injured leg felt well enough that he happily discarded the poultice.

Thomas had overslept, but he hoped the townspeople would forgive him for the late start. He knew that each day the townspeople awoke to a fearful future. They were depending on him. But he was so tired.

And he was dirty. *I smell more like the foul poultice than like a human*, he admitted to himself. It was time to stonewash some of his clothing. Following the advice he had given to Horsetender, he decided to clean himself up, as well. He washed some of his most disgusting-smelling clothes and laid them out on the rock face to dry. He then waded into the dark pool and began to cleanse himself.

The water was cold but refreshing, and he felt his energy return. He began to truly relax for the first time in many days and became a bit careless with his footing. The rock floor of the pool was covered with moss and was slippery in spots. Thomas stepped onto one of the mossy spots, lost his balance, and tumbled into the deep center of the pool.

He floundered, fighting to keep his head up and get to shallower water. But his lack of swimming ability turned his efforts into vain splashing. He did get close enough to the shallow area to reach the bottom with his hands, but there was nothing to grasp. His desperate reach served only to make him drift back toward the center of the pool.

Thomas felt himself beginning to tire. Finally, energy spent, he slipped below the surface of the water. He weakly thrashed his arms for a few moments then all became quiet. As he drifted toward the bottom of the pool, he looked up at the mirror-like surface that seemed so close. He could see his last bubbles of breath rise and pop on the surface. It looked beautiful.

His mind was telling him, *A little rest will be fine. Just one deep breath will do it.* His last thoughts before all went black were of Rachael and Hope. Had he done for them everything he could? Then he was waving goodbye to his family. Thomas barely noticed a shadow cover the surface. He never felt the disturbance in the water, which produced a pressure wave that bounced him off the rocky bottom. It felt good to let go and finally rest . . .

Thomas awoke lying face down at the edge of the pool. His trousers were soaking wet, and he was choking up water. *How did I get out of the water?* He had been fighting for air and had lost, but somehow . . . here he was. He lay in the warm, late-morning sun for some time before gathering enough strength to raise himself on one elbow and look around. He was alone.

The clothes he had laid out earlier were dry. The ordeal over; Thomas felt foolish for carelessly wading into the pool. He had no explanation for his miraculous escape but thanked a providential Maker again for his good fortune.

He considered resting longer and rolled over. He noticed a solitary, red-edged wildflower protruding from the moss in the otherwise barren landscape. Thoughts of his wife and daughter's daily pilgrimage to the northern ridge to leave a flower for him flooded back. This gave him the encouragement he needed to keep going.

The previous evening he had been so taken with the southern view that he completely forgot about the direction he was headed. He walked to a north-facing ledge and stood gazing from its perch. Far below, Thomas saw a beautiful green valley. It stretched into the distance, where it was veiled by heavy morning mist.

He could see warm springs running into the valley. They left steamy trails winding through the cultivated land. To his right he saw a wide path hewn from the granite. It appeared to switch back and forth as it ran down to the forested foothills.

Thomas repacked his rucksack and followed the broad path down the north side of the forbidding mountains. He marveled at the path's handiwork and stopped to feel the smooth cuts that ran deeply into the hard rock.

The descent, though easier, was long and took the entire day. Thomas found himself completely spent once again. His knees and thighs burned from the stress of the long downhill trek. By the time he arrived at the forested foothills, it was too late to explore the valley. He found a spacious clearing and prepared a large fire to ward off whatever animals roamed the northern side of the mountain.

With darkness closing in, Thomas determined to get a good rest before entering the valley that opened before him. He laid out his bedroll near the fire at the base of the great mountain path. He heard no wolves howling during the night, which greatly comforted him. *Tomorrow will be an interesting day,* he thought as he fell into an unconscious rest.

Little did he know that the next morning would bring a startling discovery.

Land of Giants

THOMAS WAS AWAKENED by a loud grunt. He rubbed the sleep from his eyes and discovered two huge feet standing astride his burned-out campfire. They were attached to legs that looked as large as tree trunks.

Before the morning fog cleared from his head, a booming voice announced, "I am Mountainbiter, carver of wide mountain paths and shaper of stone. We do not welcome outsiders here. What brings you to the edge of our land?" The giant looked menacing as he towered above Thomas, stone-faced. He held a great iron hammer in one hand and a chisel the size of a small tree trunk in the other.

Thomas was always surprised at the wide variety of physical build and look of giants. Each seemed to have been made from a truly unique mold. Mountainbiter's face was tanned and weathered, whereas Forestmaster was overly fair. The giant standing over him had short, dark-brown, curly hair. Forestmaster's hair was much longer, red, and wavy.

Mountainbiter did not appear to be in a mood to sit down and eat biscuits or talk about farming.

Thomas jumped to his feet with his hunting knife at the ready. He did not feel too threatened but his instincts took over. He knew this volume and tone of voice was not unusual for a giant. Nevertheless, it was not a pleasant way for anyone to be awakened from a deep, satisfying sleep.

He scanned the giant before him. Mountainbiter was not as tall as Forestmaster, but his shoulders and back were broader. His muscles rippled from the tops of his biceps to his fingertips. He was powerful—even by giant standards.

"I come in search of those who for as long as time is remembered worked side-by-side with us in our land," Thomas said, "Yet they lately have disappeared, and the townsfolk are distressed. There is much work to be done. They find it overwhelming without their giant friends."

Mountainbiter gave a great laugh that shook the ground and said, "We have heard of such difficulties before, but seldom has anyone braved the long trek and climbed the great mountain to question our actions."

"Giants leave a trail that is easy to find but nearly impossible to follow," Thomas replied.

Mountainbiter roared a great laugh again. He seemed a jolly fellow. "You have walked in the footsteps of giants," he said. "You have crossed the great barrier and arrived where no one thought possible. This is a story worth hearing and telling."

Thomas felt less anxious now. He sheathed his knife and said, "I am friend to Forestmaster and have worked many years by his side, as did my fathers before me. I seek my friend to learn the purpose of the giants' departure."

Mountainbiter gave him a sympathetic look. "I am sorry, but our law is clear. No outsiders may enter our land unless they have been invited. Have you evidence of such an invitation?"

Thomas held out his open palms and shook his head in defeat. He had no invitation, and he could not hope to force his way past

Mountainbiter. His knees lost their strength, and he fell onto a stump near his bedroll. "I have nothing but the good faith and hope of my people. I have traveled far and through many trials to arrive at your borders. Does this not count for something?"

"I am truly sorry that you cannot pass farther into our lands," Mountainbiter said. "I promise that Forestmaster will hear of your effort to reach him. Perhaps something may come of it. But I am sorrier still that I will not hear of your travels. I will walk with you to the base of the wide mountain trail and see you safely back to your side of the—" The giant stopped in mid-sentence and stared at the ground near the bedroll. He picked up the gnarled staff. "But you *do* have an invitation," he said, smiling. "Why didn't you say so?"

"This old staff?" said Thomas in confusion.

"Of course," said the giant. "He who possesses this staff has demonstrated the quality of his heart and the worthiness of his purpose to one well trusted by the giant people. Such a gift is never given lightly. It tells all we need to know of your integrity and goodness."

The giant put his massive hand to his head as if in deep thought and said, "If it is Forestmaster you seek, then to Forestmaster you must go. I will take you to him. Perhaps on the way you can give me a good story to tell." With that he lifted the young man, sat him on his right shoulder, and strode off at what was a casual walk for a giant. In reality, a galloping horse could hardly have kept pace.

Thomas bounced up and down on Mountainbiter's shoulder and struggled to keep his balance and take in the marvelous countryside. Every bouncing step filled him with wonder. There were giants of all shapes and sizes traveling along the wide path.

It was not only the variety of giants that caught his imagination; it was the land itself. Thomas had never seen trees so tall with trunks so thick or crops so huge and plentiful. He asked the giant how such bounty had come to be.

"The fields are all under the care of an extraordinary giant named Loamcarver. She has many apprentices, some of whom are visible in the fields," Mountainbiter explained.

Thomas saw grapes the size of a man's head, ears of corn that could fill his cottage doorway, and melons larger than any of the wagons in his village. The fields, he learned, were watered by a vast canal system built and maintained by an ingenious giant named—quite aptly—Rainbender.

The most amazing sights of all were the animals—herds of horses, cows, goats, and others, all of enormous sizes. Mountainbiter explained that Herdminder had quite a number of giants dedicated to the proper care and feeding of these great beasts. Thomas wondered if this was the group with whom Horsetender had labored.

As their travel continued, Thomas asked, "You talked about the old man who gave me the staff as one who is known and trusted by the giants. Who is he?"

"Sometimes those who are 'The One' in a village in which the giants have labored are taken with the giants when they complete their service," Mountainbiter explained. "These are then set to watch the many approaches to the Land of Giants and ensure that comings and goings are monitored. Each is referred to as a 'Forest Ward' and watched over by his companion giant."

This made sense to Thomas but he was still curious. "Where did the old man come from?"

"Years ago, the Forest Ward you met lived in a town hundreds of leagues distant, near the great southern sea to which the eastern river runs. His village was in great need just as your town was. Who he was is not as important as what he has become. He, like you, accepted a great task—to seek out the giants."

Mountainbiter paused to say "hello" to a stout giant placing huge melons in a wagon then resumed his tale. "The giants' involvement with that town was shorter than with yours. With its completion, he accepted a responsibility to monitor 'The One' as he or she journeyed from each village. He is a master at testing the size of one's heart, as he did yours. This was necessary to determine the sincerity of the request by 'The One' and the nature of the giant people's response. The size of a person's heart, as you will learn, is most important to the giant people."

"So his visit was a test, and his staff marked my passage of it?" Thomas asked.

"You have much to learn, but you are here, after all, with the staff. That is all I need to know. The greatest tests in life are not usually announced as such, nor do they require some great or noble sacrifice or act. The greatest tests are found in the small choices, acts, and events that combine to create great and important results."

The giant explained that Thomas' bravery was never in question, but his compassion and capacity to trust needed to be proven. Their conversation continued until midday, when they approached a stand of the largest trees Thomas had ever seen, with heights beyond the overhanging clouds. A side road disappeared into the vast wooden grove. It wandered as if bending to the desire of the trees for space. Mountainbiter slowed to the pace of a trotting horse.

Just before the trail disappeared into the forest, Thomas saw a large building with dark smoke billowing from a hole in its roof. "What place is this?" he asked.

Mountainbiter, clearly warmed to the companionship of his small friend, said, "This is our blacksmith, Bladesmelter. He makes the finest tools and blades in the world. I thought I saw something familiar in the workmanship of that pinprick of a blade you pulled on me when I startled you from sleep this morning. Come, let me introduce you to the master of this mighty forge."

There was no door, only a wide opening through which Mountainbiter entered the blacksmith's shop. The heat from the massive forge was intense. The clanging of metal on metal filled the shop.

As they rounded the enormous hearth, Thomas caught his first glimpse of Bladesmelter. Mountainbiter lowered Thomas from his shoulder and set him behind one of the large anvils, out of sight. "Stay here and do not reveal yourself," the giant said. "We will have a bit of fun with the blacksmith!"

Thomas sensed a practical joke in the works. He could not resist peeking around the corner of the anvil. Bladesmelter was a giant, and everything about him was large and impressive. But no giant Thomas had ever met had arms as massively muscled as did the blacksmith.

Looking up from his work, Bladesmelter's sooty face broke into a white-toothed smile that stretched from ear to ear. "Hello, my rock-carving friend. What brings you to my shop today? Have you lost one of your fine chisels again?"

"No, I can account for them all save the one I loaned to Earth-watcher a couple of days ago," said Mountainbiter. "The rest are safe in my pouch. But I do have a curiosity you may be able to help me with. It regards a blade you may be familiar with, made long ago."

"I remember every one of my creations, my friend," Bladesmelter said with confidence. "If the blade was made here, I will tell you its story."

Mountainbiter lifted Thomas from behind the anvil and set him on the hearth in front of Bladesmelter.

"Hmmm . . . it does not appear to be one of my tools, Mountainbiter. You jest with me, for this is merely a human man of average workmanship," said Bladesmelter with a booming laugh. Mountainbiter too was laughing. It took several moments before they ceased their jovial roars.

Mountainbiter regained control and turned to the young man. "Thomas, show the blacksmith your blade."

Thomas pulled the knife from its scabbard and laid it—handle first—in the blacksmith's hand.

Bladesmelter eyed it carefully and turned it over. He smiled. "Yes, I remember this well. I presented it to the last human to visit my shop. Oh, but it has been a long time. His name was also Thomas, and a brave young man he was."

A thousand questions rushed into Thomas' mind as the giant continued. "Perhaps it has been a hundred years now, but I remember the day clearly. Forestmaster brought him by as the giants were preparing to leave for a distant human town from which this man had ventured. They were to help a lost people find themselves again. Yes, I believe that was the purpose of his coming to our land in the first place, to ask for such help."

Thomas knew his third great-grandfather had traveled the wild world. However, he had no idea that he had come to the Land of Giants. He said, louder than he intended, "That was surely my kin! I bear his name and have heard that he traveled the wild lands as a young man."

Bladesmelter became serious. "Use your gift wisely, my young friend. This blade has been wielded by the bravest of men. All those who carry the blade of a giant must respect the responsibility that goes with it. Now, you have your answer and I sense your journey is urgent. It is best if you be on your way."

Thomas could think of nothing to say but "thank you" and "I will do my best" as Mountainbiter dutifully placed him back on his shoulder. They each gave a cheerful wave and turned to walk out of the shop.

Bladesmelter called to them as they crossed the threshold. "My young fellow, apparently your family has more than one brave adventurer. This merits another gift from my forge. You may find it one day when you need it most but expect it least."

Thomas handled the knife with newfound reverence. He pondered the blacksmith's words as Mountainbiter strode across the yard and toward the side road that would take them deep into the massive forest.

The trees looked larger now that he was among them than when they appeared from a distance. Mountainbiter walked purposefully, for there were no other giants on this path to distract him. As they walked, Thomas related the story of his journey. Mountainbiter listened intently.

It is very difficult to judge distance from the shoulder of a fast-moving giant, Thomas realized. He guessed they had traveled into the forest twice as far as the walk to his fields each morning. He was looking forward to seeing Forestmaster and began to grow impatient. "Are we far from the place where we will find my friend?" he called out.

"We are not only close, we are here," Mountainbiter replied.

They rounded one last bend and saw what looked to be a fine lodge. Its sides were constructed of broad tree trunks, each the thickness of the captain of the guard on his great, white stallion. A perfectly laid stone walkway led up to the lodge and ended with two huge flagstone steps at the door.

Mountainbiter strode up the stone walkway, stopped on the flagstone step, and gave a thunderous pounding on the door. Before the knock's echo had faded, Thomas heard shuffling noises, the sound of furniture toppling, and then the click of a great latch. The door opened and Thomas saw the familiar face of Forestmaster. His heart leaped in response.

"What have we here?" asked the giant.

Mountainbiter told him of his errand. He lifted the young man from his shoulder and lowered him to the great flagstone step. Forestmaster gazed with respect at his young friend, and with a great, booming laugh, he said, "You have come far and must rest and eat. Then I will give you the answers you seek."

Forestmaster thanked Mountainbiter for assisting Thomas and sent him on his way. Thomas called a thank-you to him, as well.

Mountainbiter turned at the end of the stone walk. "You have honored me this day. I have a great story to tell. I shall always remember the day I met, walked, and spoke with 'The One.'"

He was awake! he thought. He lay still on the bed and scanned the room. Everything about it was huge. He coughed. His lungs seemed to be filled with water. He coughed over and over until his side hurt and he thought his insides would surely come up the next time. Aiden felt the bed shake and a huge giant of a man entered the room.

"It is a miracle, after all these days you are awake. Welcome to my home, I am called Healthmender," said the huge figure.

"Where am I? I was on the river and went under," Aiden questioned in between coughs.

"You are in the Land of Giants. You were brought here by a giant that was assigned to watch over you. His name is Needbringer. He will be very happy to hear you are awake."

Aiden felt extremely weak and could barely keep his eyes open. His body ached and his lungs gurgled with liquid making it hard to breath. "What is wrong with me?"

"You nearly drowned in the river and were pulled from the bottom by Needbringer. You have been unconscious on this bed for almost three weeks. You are still not well. Your chest is full of liquid that I fear carries something that is attacking your body. You cough up much of the liquid but more appears to take its place. I have given you a poultice that has helped some but you remain far from well. You must rest here. We will try to help you gain your strength back," counseled Healthminder.

Remembering the reason for his journey Aiden asked, "What of my town. Can the giant people help?"

"Your message has been delivered and a response is being considered. You are a brave lad. I am honored to have you in my home. Now rest and we will see what the poultice can do."

Aiden's eyes closed heavily even while his mind began to form new questions. Then he suddenly felt at ease in the realization that his mission had been successful. The giants were considering the plight of his town on the slopes of the western mountains. He allowed himself to sink back into the deep comfortable bed. He could do no more today. Tomorrow he would try again.

Questions and Answers

ORESTMASTER LED THOMAS inside and made space for him on the great wooden table. His chair was a wooden spool of yarn; a piece of firewood served as a table, with a shiny belt buckle as his plate. Thomas thought the room looked large enough to fit his entire cottage. Bare logs with the bark stripped off formed the walls. The logs fit together so tightly that he imagined no draft seeped through, not even on the windiest night.

Forestmaster righted the chair he had evidently knocked over at Mountainbiter's rapping then sat down across from Thomas. Forestmaster's wife, Threadweaver, brought drink and food from the kitchen and set it before Thomas. She inquired about Rachael and Hope, and listened as Thomas related the confusion and fear that reigned in town. Threadweaver shared a knowing look with her husband and left the two alone, retiring to the kitchen.

With his hunting knife, Thomas cut a slice from the largest chunk of beef he had ever seen. He dipped his flask into the giant's great mug of water to wash the delicious roast down. The mug was large enough to serve as a fine watering trough for several horses.

Forestmaster broke the silence first. "Your name was spoken in this house only this morning, my friend."

Thomas paused in his slicing of another slab of beef. "How can this be?"

"Someone stopped by who is apparently a new friend of yours," the giant replied respectfully. "I had not seen him for many years. He is called Horsetender."

"How did your conversation go with him?" Thomas asked, curious and hopeful.

Forestmaster smiled. "Horsetender has been absent from our people for a long time. He was hesitant about coming back even though he clearly felt it was the right thing to do. He said a great man taught him that hope can be a powerful tool . . . and so it was." His smile grew wider. "You have done a good and selfless thing, my young friend. Such an act is worthy of even the greatest of giants."

Thomas didn't know how to respond, but he was glad Horsetender had returned to his people. "What will he do now?" he asked.

"The first step is the hardest but must be taken," Forestmaster responded thoughtfully. "It is important that Horsetender has reached out and found a hand of welcome. He will now need to find his place again and relearn what makes the heart of a giant. This will require change."

"I hope he can do it," said Thomas.

"You have given him a reason and a way to rebuild his faith and purpose. Of course he must continue to take each step himself. But I believe he can do it, and there are many who will help. We are not merely giants but are a 'giant people,' and as such we care for each other. Horsetender will find many willing to help if he will allow it. This is a lesson all giants must learn."

The rest of the meal passed in silence. After a time, Threadweaver brought Thomas one of her pin cushions, with the pins removed. He relaxed, using it as a pillow, as they continued their conversation.

"Now, what urgent matter brings my young friend so far and through so much peril?" Forestmaster asked.

Thomas quickly blurted out a question of his own. "Why did you leave us?"

"It was time for us to move on," answered the giant.

"What do you mean by *that*?" Thomas asked. His voice carried an edge he had not intended to reveal.

The giant seemed not to notice his young friend's tone. He spoke quietly, especially for one so large. "We did all that was necessary. It is now time for the people of your town to become something more."

"Something more than *what*?" Thomas exclaimed, shaking his head. "You do not answer my questions. You only add confusion."

The giant looked about the room as if seeking a key to understanding for his young friend. "A giant is not measured by his stature, my friend," he said patiently. "A true giant is measured by the size of his *heart*."

Oh, now we're really *getting somewhere*, thought Thomas sarcastically. *What does the size of a giant's heart have to do with why you left?*

As if reading his thoughts, the giant continued. "The size of one's heart is measured by his courage to face trials and by the collective size of all those hearts and souls whom he has loved more than self. This is what Horsetender had forgotten."

A sliver of understanding was beginning to dawn on Thomas. "I understand the value of what you speak. But what does this have to do with the giants leaving our town? We need you."

Compassion was written deeply on the giant's face. A great tear formed in his eye. He turned to see Threadweaver standing in the doorway. They nodded to each other, as if the time had come to do something they had long discussed.

Forestmaster turned back to his small friend. "Before I answer, you must understand something of our beginnings," he said with reverence. "The race of giants has tilled the ground and tended the forests and wildlife in this valley since beyond memory. From our beginnings in the dim past we have loved the earth and its wonderful fruits and beauty.

"Because of this great love we desired to grow to maturity and remain without natural death so that we could always watch over the work of our Maker's hands. The greatest of all the giants, Sonspeaker, sought out Him whose name we call Worldmaker and obtained such a promise. Worldmaker, whom humankind has named differently, required a promise in return."

Forestmaster took a deep breath and continued. "The giants, Sonspeaker was told, must love and serve all people and teach them the importance of this love borne of selfless service. By doing so, they would thus unfold to humankind the secret of becoming something more than they otherwise would have been. This we have done for thousands of years, most recently with your people."

"But we are not giants!" Thomas cried. "We are small and afraid and at the mercy of a dangerous world and fearsome elements."

"Hmmm . . . you are more than you imagine, my friend," Forestmaster said kindly. "And your people are also more than they realize. How would you ever come to know this for yourselves if the giants were always with you?"

The light of understanding had begun to shine a bit brighter for Thomas. "So, leaving was always known to you? It was meant to teach us something we could not otherwise learn?"

"Yes, you begin to see more clearly," said the giant. "You begin to see with your eyes *and* with your heart."

"Why didn't you warn us you were going to leave? Or your true purpose in laboring at our side?" Thomas asked, thinking he had found a flaw in the giant's story.

"Well, my friend, that would have changed everything. It is the preparation for something you cannot clearly see that develops faith. It is the sudden, dramatic change with an uncertain outcome that most properly tests it. That is why you could not be allowed to clearly see 'The Way of Things,' as we call it."

The giant went on. "Knowing we would be leaving could easily have been an overwhelming distraction. It might have produced anxiety that would slow or divert your natural growth and maturity as a people. Perhaps even stop it. Fear can do that, you know. But faith, once developed and carefully nurtured, is a most powerful tool."

"Why then, if we have grown so much, is there such great commotion and fear among my people?" Thomas inquired, truly open to learning now.

"Your people have worked hard. They are good and faithful. However, they are not yet sufficiently wise. They have always been able to turn to us for solutions to their greatest problems. The time for first lessons is past. It is now time for understanding and wisdom. You are a fine example of that. Look what you have accomplished in coming here. It is a courageous feat."

The giant paused. He caught his wife's gaze from the doorway and a new idea seemed to dawn in his countenance. "But . . . it is more than that. It is a selfless sacrifice for your people. There must always be 'One.' This is The Way of Things, and you are not the first in your family, are you?"

The young man understood the giant's point and described his visit with Bladesmelter.

The giant listened with great interest then nodded. "No product of Bladesmelter's forge is ever given lightly. The journey that brought you here has honored your family and Bladesmelter. Before we continue I would like you to tell me of your great adventures. The giants will tell this story around their hearths for a hundred years."

Thomas shared the story of his journey. Forestmaster listened and nodded often, as if gaps in other conversations were now neatly filled in. Midday turned to afternoon, and one last question remained on Thomas' mind. He turned the conversation back to the purpose of his quest. "You say that the giants leaving our lands was part of 'The Way of Things.' But how will we manage without you?"

The giant stood, gave a ceremonial bow, and said, "My friend, *you* are the answer to that question."

The Grand Council

"**I** AM THE answer? How can that be?" Thomas felt completely bewildered.

Just as the giant was about to respond, a pounding came at the door. Forestmaster rose and opened the door. From his vantage point, Thomas could see he was talking to a shorter giant, a little over half Forestmaster's height. He had straw-colored hair, strong legs, and a nimble build—if that were possible to say of a giant.

The smaller giant was dressed in forest green and carried a long, intricately carved walking stick. The two giants gave a hearty laugh at one point in their conversation. The smaller one waved hello to Thomas, still chuckling. Then their talk turned serious and quiet.

The conversation ended and goodbyes said. Forestmaster returned to the table and sat down.

"I have just received important news from Earthwatcher. He is responsible for observing the towns from which we giants have recently removed," he explained. "Earthwatcher's current assignment is your village, Thomas. He is also responsible for stepping in—but only in moments of urgent need—to protect and assist The One from each village."

"Are you saying he helped me?" asked Thomas.

"Yes, my young friend. How do you think you pulled yourself out of a mud-filled hole when the rope lay loose on the ground? Why do you believe the wolves waited so long to attack? Why didn't they strike you while you slept? When they finally *did* attack, how do you think the steps in the granite face got there?" Forestmaster paused. "Do you think it is a coincidence that a rock fell from the mountain just as the wolves had you? Have you not wondered how you suddenly awoke on the edge of the pool instead of being drowned?

"Earthwatcher's responsibilities are vital. He does not intervene unless there is no other way. Dealing with and overcoming difficulties, as you did in the dry plain, is the best teacher," Forestmaster continued with a serious look. "Even with his help, the matter with the wolves was a close one. Earthwatcher asks your forgiveness because his intervention came almost too late. He also is sorry it took so long to pull you from the pool. Earthwatcher never imagined you would be foolish enough to go for a swim when you have not the skill."

"I know. It was both foolish and embarrassing and certainly not Earthwatcher's failing," said Thomas with a blush of embarrassment.

The giant's face widened into a toothy smile and he chuckled. "I would have given much to have seen the muddy, drowned rat of a man who climbed out of that hole in the storm. Earthwatcher described it quite well, but I shall have to live with the picture in my mind only."

"Please tell Earthwatcher thank you," Thomas said, "for I surely would have perished had he not shadowed my path. His intervention with the wolves came in time, and the effect of the injury to my leg is past." He paused. "Is there any news, then, from my town?"

Forestmaster nodded. "A great change is occurring among your people. Earthwatcher suggests it would be wise for you to return home. However, it is too late to begin the journey today. We could not get over the great barrier before dark," he explained. "It is unwise even for giants to attempt to climb the great barrier in the dark so we will begin at first light tomorrow morning."

The giant smiled. "It is fortunate you are here this evening. Sonspeaker has called a meeting of the Grand Council, and you are invited to attend a portion of it. Our conversation and further answers to your questions can wait until morning, my friend. There will be plenty of time."

It was late in the afternoon when Forestmaster kissed Thread-weaver goodbye. With Thomas on his shoulder, he walked with brisk giant steps through the winding forest path to the northern edge. There the land opened up into a large, round clearing the size of one of Thomas' fields. The entire area was covered in short grass. An enormous fire pit took up the center of the clearing. Large spits of meat were roasting over the fire. It smelled wonderful.

The ground curved up into a bowl that appeared to accommodate seating for much larger giant meetings. There were eight giant-sized stools surrounding the fire, all of equal size. Thomas counted six giants sitting on the stools. They appeared deep in discussion. Two stools stood empty, apparently waiting to be filled by Forestmaster and Thomas. They were the last to arrive. Thomas recognized three of the giants: Earthwatcher, Mountainbiter, and Bladesmelter.

The other three giants were new to him. As they walked from the edge of the clearing toward the gathering, Forestmaster pointed out Loamcarver. She was a female giant of huge stature at least a head taller than Forestmaster. Her muscles were less defined but there was real strength in her frame. Her long, shining blond hair hung almost to her waist in a braided ponytail.

"She represents the needs of all those who tend and care for the Land of Giants," Forestmaster told Thomas. "Her input is important whenever giants are selected to serve villages out in the wide world. She also provisions those tasked with the responsibility of serving humans."

Thomas nodded.

"Earthwatcher, as I told you already, observes the doings of the towns we have departed from," the giant continued. "He probably has already given his report on your village. Bladesmelter provides the tools, plows, and equipment for this land. His tools are also important to those serving humans. His advice is often sought when a plan for a new village is presented.

"Mountainbiter is not usually in attendance. However, he has been invited today to provide an objective report on the One who entered our land this morning."

"You mean me?" said Thomas.

"Yes," Forestmaster said, smiling. "No one enjoys telling a good tale more or is better at it than Mountainbiter."

"What is *your* purpose here at the Grand Council?" Thomas asked.

"Oh, that is easy. I was the leader of the most recent village effort in which our labors were completed, so I may be asked to report. If there is a new village to discuss, that may involve me as well," said the giant.

"Who are the other two giants, and what purpose do they serve here?" asked Thomas.

"The thin, wiry giant is named Needbringer. If he is present, it means another village might be in difficulty. He may have asked the Council if the village can be helped and, if so, what is needed."

Needbringer looked more like a tall, skinny sapling than a giant. He had dark-brown hair that stuck straight up. He also had a long, pointed nose and an even longer face. His ears seemed twice the size necessary to fit his head.

"Do not be deceived by his slight build," warned Forestmaster. "There are many thousands of lost souls who have found themselves because of Needbringer's watchful eye. His love for the earth and its people is deeper than any but Sonspeaker himself."

Thomas turned to the last of the giants, one who did not appear to be the tallest or the strongest. But he was handsomely built and only slightly shorter than Forestmaster. His skin was a rich earthy tone. His long, white hair flowed several inches past his shoulders. It matched the white mustache that curved around his mouth and into a beard, which made him look truly regal.

He stood dressed in a flowing white robe worn over a simple brown tunic. There was nothing particular about him that shouted "leader," but his presence effortlessly commanded the group's attention.

He held a staff of dark-brown hardwood that stood well above his head. Polished to a perfect finish, the fire reflecting off the staff made it appear to glow. As they approached the group, Thomas noticed the giant's watchful green eyes that surely missed nothing.

"That is Sonspeaker," said Forestmaster with deep respect. "We have no kings or mayors here. Our leader is measured by the size of his heart. Sonspeaker's deep and unconditional love for the giant people as well as for the human race and the earth itself is unmatched. We all have our responsibilities. Sonspeaker sees and hears all our joys and trials. He unites us in a hope for the future that adds real purpose to our lives." They covered the remaining distance to the gathering.

Sonspeaker addressed them first. "Hello, my old friend. I understand you have received an unusual visitor this day, and he has come to join us in our Council."

"This is true," Forestmaster said. He lifted Thomas from his shoulder and placed him gently on the nearest stool. The giants who had been conversing among themselves ceased talking. They looked at Thomas with what appeared to be respect and awe.

"I have told his story," said Mountainbiter. "His courage, faith, and the size of his heart far exceed his stature."

"Yes," added Earthwatcher. "This One may be the bravest to venture to our land since he who bore the same name long ago."

"But, my friends, we have an urgent need that must be discussed first," said Needbringer. "The decision cannot long be delayed."

"You are right," replied Sonspeaker. "Let us get to the heart of the matter. Please resume your seats. Forestmaster, you and The One may sit here." He motioned to the stools nearest him.

Then Sonspeaker spoke again. "Forestmaster, we have an urgent need reported from one of the villages in the foothills of the far western mountains. For an entire generation, the people of that village have become increasingly obsessed with games of chance and pursuits that distract them from their families and duties. Their leaders have become consumed with greed and force their will upon the people. Their crops lay wasting in the fields because too many of the young men and women engage in riotous behavior. They spend their treasure on things of no value.

"The children wander unsupervised, slip into all manner of mischief, and are developing an attitude of skepticism and doubt rather than hope and faith. They are unprepared for the difficulties ahead and do little to develop those who are to come."

Sonspeaker drew a deep breath and continued. "The town is not without hope, but those who see clearly are few and their influence dwindles. There was *One* who ventured from the town in search of our land. Unfortunately, his small craft broke apart in the rain-swollen river. Needbringer rescued him. The One was seriously injured and remains unconscious. He currently rests in the home of Healthmender, who is tending his injuries. I am told he may recover in time. What are the thoughts of the Council?"

"I stopped by just prior to the meeting and was informed the young man has awakened. But he has contracted a serious illness that fills his chest with liquid and threatens to drown him from within," commented Needbringer.

"It is good to hear he is conscious. He could not be in better hands. Now let us continue considering the plight of his town," said Sonspeaker.

"We should determine our ability to make a difference," said Bladesmelter. "It is a long journey to the western mountains if the townsfolk are unwilling to accept what we offer."

"Yes, you are right. We cannot force our involvement on a community. Our participation must be freely chosen by those we serve or it is not service at all but tyranny," reasoned Forestmaster, "and contrary to The Way of Things."

"What if the people will not listen or refuse to understand?" asked Thomas.

All faces turned to Sonspeaker as he responded. "You ask a question that has troubled giants for many generations. We have had towns reject our help out of pride or overwhelming selfishness. Sometimes they cannot see the truth of their situation through their own eyes. While The Way of Things is the only path worth taking, it is not an easy one. Other paths may seem easier at first, but as Horsetender has shared with you, they lead to *nothing*."

"Why would people choose *nothing* over growth, bitterness over accomplishment, or sadness over joy?" Thomas persisted.

"Because selfishness, self-indulgence, and useless distraction pretend to be freedom at first. Only later are they revealed as a prison that increasingly restricts the lives of those entrapped," Sonspeaker said sadly. "Often they cannot see clearly until it captures them."

"We are bound to try and see what the people desire," Needbringer said encouragingly. "I have observed these people for some time. I believe there is good in them, which gives me hope that they will respond positively to our invitation."

"I can take a small advance group to assess the situation and meet with the town's leaders," Forestmaster offered. "Certainly, we cannot help any who do not wish to be helped. Yet, perhaps there are enough who seek to be more than they have become." He looked at Thomas. "I have promised to accompany this young man back to his village. I can then meet with the advance group before they arrive at the western village."

"That is good," Sonspeaker said, looking relieved. "Needbringer, can you lead the advance group until Forestmaster arrives?"

"I will gladly help as I can," said Needbringer.

Forestmaster nodded his agreement. They discussed the details of provisions and tools, and more was said about the state of the people in the western village. The fire burned low while they worked out the details and decided who would be in the advance group.

With everything settled and the evening long spent, Sonspeaker turned to Thomas. "I understand you have come here for answers. But it seems you have also brought a great gift to one of our people."

Thomas was confused and looked at Sonspeaker.

"I speak of the great gift you call 'godly hope' that you have given to our long-lost friend Horsetender," Sonspeaker explained. "This is no trivial act, Thomas. It will be spoken of throughout our land for many years. We have agreed that your name will be written in the ledger of our people as one of the 'Giants of the Land,'" he said with a flourish of his hand.

The other giants stood and bowed in respect.

"Our business is now complete this evening," Sonspeaker said, "but Thomas has come to our land with many questions. Let us hear and answer one of them."

Thomas had waited for this opportunity all evening. He had so many questions swirling in his mind it was difficult to choose. He thought for a moment then settled on the question he and Forestmaster had discussed before Earthwatcher had come to the door. "Why do you say that *I* am the answer to the question?"

The giants glanced from Sonspeaker to Forestmaster then back to Sonspeaker, as if this were the weightiest question Thomas could have posed. Sonspeaker adjusted his position on the large stool nearest the ebbing flames and said, "The answer you seek depends on your growth and what that allows you to give. Your people have a great need right now, and you can only give what you have. But you have more than you know. You have much more than you possessed a few weeks ago."

Thomas began to feel frustrated with riddles again and tried to stay focused. "Can you speak plainly, so that one who is still trying to appreciate what his path has produced may understand?"

"Certainly," said a new voice from his right. It was Loamcarver. She continued the thought with a different emphasis. "You decide how much of the question you can answer by your preparation and training, your insight and growth, and by whom you have become. Your people have a question. What is it?"

Thomas thought for a moment. "Our most important question is, 'What do we do if the giants never come back?'"

"Precisely," said Loamcarver. "Think, Thomas, because this is also *your* greatest question. How are *you* the answer to that question? How are *you* the answer to *your* own question about what to do?"

Then it dawned on Thomas like a distant light seen by a lone traveler on a dark night. He knew the answer as the traveler could see the distant light. But like the traveler, Thomas did not yet know how to reach it.

"We all have the same question about what to do. We are each the answer to our own question," Thomas reasoned aloud. "This means . . . we exercise our faith to turn hope into action, and we build a future with our own hands."

The giants cheered and nodded. Several commented with "Well done!" and "You've got it!" and "What an amazing one he is!" before they quieted down.

Sonspeaker spoke once more that special evening—an evening Thomas would always remember. "Thomas, you have discovered the key but have yet to understand the lock in which it is used. The lock this key opens will be illuminated for you by Forestmaster as you travel to your village. But remember, knowing *you* are the best answer to *your* challenges and questions must be accompanied by knowledge of how to become that answer. A person who pursues being nothing cannot become the answer to any worthwhile question. Ponder that thought this evening, for your destiny is almost upon you. There is little time to prepare."

Sonspeaker paused for a moment and Thomas allowed Sonspeaker's profound advice to sink deeply into his soul. Then Sonspeaker spoke again. "You will always be welcome here, for you are one of us now. We shall honor your name, but you have also earned another name by which you will be known among the giants. I name you Thomas Hopegiver. We would choose to spend many days in your company but, as with any giant, you are needed elsewhere."

The Way Home

THE WALK BACK to the lodge after the Council ended seemed long. Thomas kept falling asleep on Forestmaster's shoulder. He would have fallen off twice had the giant not held him firmly in place. Later, Thomas slept on the floor in a comfortable bed Threadweaver had made for him. It consisted of a corner of one of their blankets tucked around him until he could barely see out.

There was no further conversation that night. It was late, and they needed to make an early start in the morning. Forestmaster had agreed to accompany him as far as the hilly ridge north of his town. They could discuss Thomas' questions on the way.

The return home went much quicker than Thomas' journey to the Land of Giants. Riding on the shoulder of a giant makes travel far easier than hiking the rough terrain on foot, he reflected. The long hike up the wide mountain path was smooth and pleasant. Thomas noticed that the clefts of rock that seemed so far apart when he climbed the face were perfectly set for a giant's hand and footholds.

The passage went swiftly, although crossing the lake required Thomas to ride on Forestmaster's great red head. The center of the lake was deep, even for a giant. They camped only once—on the edge of the dry plain where Thomas had first heard the wolves.

While the campfire burned brightly, Forestmaster answered Thomas' questions and explained more about The Way of Things. "All people grow up with giants in their lives on whom they depend, just as the townspeople depended on their giants," he explained. "This learning environment is important in every society. But if carried too far, people tend to become overly dependent on their giants."

He sighed. "This can produce a lack of appreciation that can lead to taking much for granted. There comes a moment in every person's life when he or she discovers that the giants to whom they had always looked are gone. This can be a time of trial and sorrow. Some are unable to continue onward; their courage and heart fail them. However, if handled wisely, this can be a time of unmatched growth," the giant said.

"We have discovered that people need someone who understands the giants' true purpose, in order to help them face their fear and overcome it. The One in each village has the necessary perspective and must teach them."

Thomas felt unequal to the task of being this One in his village. He expressed his self-doubt.

Forestmaster responded with authority. "It is natural that you would have doubts, but The One cannot be forced. He or she must step forward voluntarily, as you did. Only this kind of selfless decision allows the One to endure the path to wisdom and understanding, as you have done. You have many doubts. But you know in your heart the power of hope, which leads to the exercise of faith, which in turn becomes knowledge, inner strength, and wisdom. You have felt it change you into something different, have you not?"

"I guess I *do* feel a bit different now. I have learned much that I will attempt to pass on," said Thomas. "I promise."

"That is the first step!" exclaimed the giant. "You see what I see now. You have become a man of purpose. That is an excellent start!"

Thomas slept well and unafraid of the sounds that night. When he awoke, he felt sad. He knew this was likely their last day together. He would miss his giant friend and would always remember what Forestmaster had taught him.

The rest of the trip was sheer pleasure. Thomas especially enjoyed crossing the desolate plain. The giant moved swiftly, and the lack of water was not a concern. It seemed but a moment and they were beyond the plain that had nearly cost Thomas his life a few weeks before.

The only discomfort Thomas endured was when Forestmaster strode up and down the many rolling hills and ridges beyond the plain. At one point, he asked Forestmaster to stop and allow him to rest. He needed to get over the sick, roiling feeling in his stomach from the constant up and down movement over the terrain.

Their journey from the edge of the forest to the last ridge just north of his town took most of the day. As they crested the last ridge, Thomas's eyes welled up with tears at the sight before him.

CHAPTER 14

Something Different

A ROUGH PILE of rocks was stacked at the highest point of the ridge. A beautiful yellow wildflower rose hopefully from the top. He saw other older dried flowers beside the wildflower as a testimony of his wife and daughter's daily pilgrimage.

"You see," said the giant, "there are those who have considered you their giant for a long time."

They lay down near the rock cairn to remain unseen while they observed the goings on in the valley below. Work was slow, but it was being accomplished. Trees were being felled and moved. Stones were being fitted into the unfinished fortress walls. The people were rebuilding the levee and harvesting crops.

To be certain, the work was progressing much slower than before, requiring more people to work together. The stones they moved were smaller. They felled and cut the trees into more manageable sizes. The crops left the fields in smaller loads. It had been nearly a month, but things were getting done.

"Your people no longer need giants to do their most difficult work," Forestmaster remarked.

"It will be harder and slower," said Thomas. "We will need to be satisfied with the best we can do."

"Yes, my friend," replied Forestmaster. "You are becoming wise already. Such insight will encourage hope among your people. You may find that many remain afraid. Others will become easily discouraged by the slow pace and difficult work."

The young man gazed in wonder as he realized the full impact of the giant's message. "I think I understand now. You told me we all grow up with giants in our lives, and it is true. We learn from them but also become dependent, which means our growth becomes limited. In his great wisdom, Worldmaker decreed the giants' sojourn among men would be temporary." "Sometimes"—Thomas took a long, thoughtful breath—"the giants we depend on leave our lives unexpectedly, like my father did. Such sudden changes are difficult to overcome."

He looked up at Forestmaster. "I believe the unexpected departure of the giant people is a shadow of the things that will occur in our lives. The departure of our giants is an opportunity for us to prepare for other trials yet to come. I also understand giants are not 'giants' because of their size. They become so because of the size of their heart. A giant's heart is a reflection of those they have loved and served without thought of self."

"Yes," Forestmaster said, looking pleased. "You are right. However, there is one more aspect of The Way of Things you must appreciate. After all you have learned, you now stand ready for the last lesson."

The giant's voice grew reverent, and his gaze wandered toward the sky as he spoke. "There must always be giants in the land, or the people cannot prosper and grow. When those who have learned to be giants are gone, a new generation of giants must have already been prepared to step forward and carry on. There must be One in every village to give hope, to teach, and to show the way. You, Thomas, are The One who will oversee the training of the next generation of giants in *your* village. You alone were willing to pay the price necessary to understand The Way of Things."

Forestmaster raised his hand and gestured toward the valley. "They have toiled and learned over recent weeks," he said, "but their commitment is fragile. Their hope lies in the answer they expect you to bring them upon your return. They expect you to tell them the giants are coming back."

"But . . . I do not bring the answer they *seek*," Thomas said weakly. He felt inadequate to the task ahead.

"Yes, that is true," said Forestmaster with a solemn bow. "But you bring the answer they *need*."

Thomas felt as if a great weight had settled upon his shoulders. "I cannot be a giant for all these people!" he cried.

"Ah, but you already are," responded the giant. "The people looked to you and certain others in the town for guidance during their time of great difficulty. You stepped forward when no one else did. They will come to you again for solutions as you all move forward together. It is a difficult transition, perhaps the toughest in life, but it is part of the natural course. As I said before, a giant is not measured by his physical size but rather by the size of his heart. You will help this people become giants."

"But why me? I am no one particularly special among the townspeople. There are many who seem more able," pleaded the young man.

"As you once said to your wife . . . it is because you were there and stepped forward when there was no one else. Even at that time you had already become something more than you thought you were."

"But I didn't really choose," Thomas said. "I just felt something needed to be done, and no one else came forward."

"We do not usually choose to become a giant. Others choose to see you in that role, or circumstances present opportunities. Our responses determine who will be the giants. There must be someone who steps forward to lead the way. At this time, like your ancestor before you, you have become The One for this town. All these long years working together," said Forestmaster with admiration in his voice, "I had hoped you would choose to become like him when the time came. It is not hard to see one's love, devotion, and courage working in the fields and forests side by side."

There was a pause in the conversation while Thomas allowed Forestmaster's words to sink in. He had a final, unspoken question, which the giant answered before Thomas could ask.

"There must always be giants in this land. The real key is how to recognize the responsibility that comes with it. I think you understand that now is the time to go about preparing the next generation of giants. For a generation without giants is lost. So, too, is a generation of giants who become so distracted and slothful that the next generation of giants do not develop.

"That is why we came so many years ago. Your town had a generation of giants that had forgotten who they were. They fell into wasteful and selfish pursuits, much like the town in the western foothills. They became a lost people. The next generation was spoiled, dependent, and unprepared to take their place. It takes only one lost generation before a people forgets their true potential. And so, another Thomas, long ago, sought us out and we came. It required several generations to recover. Now your people have found themselves. It will be well with you."

"It is hard to know where to start," Thomas said, feeling a spark of confidence begin to burn within.

"There will always be difficulties, but you will face them together and overcome. Your children will see you live with the heart of a giant. They will hear you teach the lessons of giants, and they will learn to do the same."

"How will I teach them what they need to know?" questioned the young man.

"Think about how you brought purpose back to Horsetender's life. The giants named you Hopegiver for a reason." Forestmaster placed his massive hand on his friend's shoulder and said, "The way you live your life will determine who you become. This example will teach them to become what they must to create their own land of giants. One day they will mourn the loss of those they loved and depended on, just as you have mourned the loss of your father. But the sun will rise the next morning and they will pick up their axes and plows and carry on the work of giants."

The Way of Things

THOMAS TRIED TO put off their parting for as long as possible. He knew he might never see his giant friend again. Each was somber as they spoke and watched the work going on in the valley below. The sun set and the streets slowly emptied.

Finally, the time came for Thomas to finish his journey. "Thank you for what you have done for my people," he told Forestmaster. "I am especially grateful for what the giant people have done for me. I will miss you terribly."

The giant knelt down to Thomas' eye level. "I will miss you, too, my friend. Your bravery has blessed all our lives. Do not despair. It may be that your family and the giants are destined to cross paths again."

With that, the giant rose to his full height and looked down at Thomas. "You, my friend, have the heart of a giant. Use it well." Forestmaster reached into his shirt pocket and pulled out the old, gnarled staff. He handed it to Thomas and said, "Take this and guard it well. You will always merit a welcome invitation in our land. But there may come a time when need requires that another travel in your footsteps."

Forestmaster turned and walked to the north without a backward glance.

Thomas watched the giant until he disappeared over the far ridge. Then he looked toward the valley—his valley—and began the last few miles of his journey home. He felt overwhelmed with fatigue. A grateful tear ran down his cheek.

He had traveled far, and the flower in his hand held the promise of a welcome return. He arrived in town long after dark. The streets were deserted and he went unheralded to his home. Thomas slipped in through the front door and found the cottage quiet and dark. He moved to the hearth and returned his bow, quiver, and knife to their honored spots.

Each had served him well on his journey. He made room for one additional item, the gnarled staff. He laid it respectfully on the ledge over the hearth. Thomas then retired upstairs to the sleeping area. He washed off many days of layered grime and quietly slipped into a bed that had never felt so soft.

Rachael stirred but remained in a deep slumber. He kissed her lightly on the cheek and whispered, "The giants are wrong, you know. *You* are the one with the heart of a giant." She slept undisturbed. Thomas lay back, stared at the ceiling, and was pleased he could hear no howling wolves.

Thomas arose far earlier than usual the next morning. He stood looking in the mirror and thought again of his father. There was still an empty place in his heart, and he longed for that absent relationship. But the dull pain that had always accompanied it was gone.

"Why is that?" he mused. The answer came strong and clear. "I now understand that Father still walks at my side."

He returned to the bedside and kissed his sleeping wife. Thomas then looked in on his daughter. Hope seemed to have new and wonderful possibilities. Today was a new day for the young man. He would have a warm breakfast waiting for his wife when she awoke. He wanted her to be the first to understand The Way of Things, for she had always been the giant in his life.

His daughter would soon begin to accompany him to the fields. She would learn how to become a giant herself. Thomas would go about his duties with a different kind of confidence, a newfound courage that told him he had become something more than he was before. He would speak with the mayor. Together they would teach the people the true nature of giants, why they had come, and why they had departed so suddenly. Most importantly, his example would be that of the One who taught his people that the giants had never really left.

Thomas walked to the front door, opened it, and stepped onto the porch. *It's going to be a beautiful day,* he thought. He noticed a finely made plow sitting to the side of the dirt walkway. Curious, he walked over to get a closer look. The plow showed fine workmanship. It would make his work in the fields go much easier.

Upon closer inspection, Thomas saw a large "B" welded into the face of the blade. A grateful smile came to his face as he realized the measure of Bladesmelter's honor. "The giants have been true to their word and have not left us helpless," he said aloud. Then he chuckled. "The blacksmith will spend many months trying to match this one."

The town was coming awake. Thomas did not want to announce his return yet. His first desire was to have a few quiet moments with his sweetheart, Rachael. They had much to discuss and even more to look forward to. Her advice would help him stay focused during what would surely be a day of many emotions.

The transition would be difficult for the town. It would take hope, faith, and the action that is inspired from both. Thomas knew in his heart that the people were already "becoming." They had begun to answer their most important questions. Life in the village would be all right. It would be immensely satisfying to watch the townsfolk become more than they were.

But that could wait awhile. Thomas turned toward the cottage and the first duty of his new life. He had a warm breakfast to make for his sweetheart and a wildflower to give his daughter. He closed the front door with a new kind of confidence. He now understood why there would always be giants in this land, and that *he* was one of them.

Hope Rises

SHE SAT ON the edge of her father's bed, holding one of his hands to her cheek. Her younger siblings were gathered nearby. She was in her mid-twenties and a mother now. Her infant son, named after his grandfather, lay cradled in her husband's left arm. Her husband stood at her side with a supportive hand on her shoulder.

She was strong and agile like her father, and she had learned to hunt and work the fields at an early age. Her long, blond hair and natural beauty were untarnished by a life that required long hours of hard work each day. Her wisdom, understanding, faith, and hope—learned from parental example—were recognized by the townspeople who sought her out often for advice.

She had cherished her quiet moments with Father and Mother over the years. They always took time to answer her questions and respond to her curiosity. Mother's passing just a year earlier had taken a heavy toll on everyone. Father was especially affected, although most people never saw it. He fought to keep his focus and continued laboring for his family and town. But the winter chill had entered his bones this year and had never left. He lay before her, his body on fire from a fever that was slowly draining away his life.

She gazed with love and gratitude upon this man who, together with his sweetheart, had spent his life in unconditional service to the people, and especially to his family. She was not old enough to remember the early days immediately after her father returned from his journey. But they had talked of it often as they walked to the fields together each morning. She knew the lessons by heart. More importantly, she lived them and knew she had become something more as a result.

It had been difficult when he had first returned. Some had become depressed and discouraged when they heard the giants would not be returning. Their faith was too weak to believe they could carry on the work and become giants themselves. But her father had been patient. With time and a core of those who recognized their own potential, the people responded and the town began to flourish again.

She didn't remember ever seeing a giant. Yet she knew what one looked like because she had lived with them her whole life.

"Are you still here, my sweetheart?" said her father weakly.

"Yes, my father, I am here."

"Have I lived as I should have?" He took a deep, slow breath. "Have your mother and I helped you, your brother, and your sister learn what you must to carry on?"

She held his hand to her lips and kissed it but had difficulty finding the words. "Father, we all have the hearts of a giant and know the responsibility that comes with it."

"I can't help feeling that there is something unfinished that I need to do," he said.

"You have served without condition or demand all your life. There is nothing more anyone in town could ask. Rest now and be at peace," she said tenderly.

Her father gave a smile of satisfaction and looked out the window to the north. "I have always loved this view. It reminds me of my giant friends, who live just over the far northern mountains." He hesitated, took a few deep breaths, and then continued, "My passing will not keep me from walking at my children's side. I will ever be there. Even now I think my sweetheart has prepared a warm welcome, and my father stretches out his hand to take me on one last walk."

He was quiet for several moments, then spoke again. "I have something for you. Please give me your hand."

His question seemed a signal to her younger sister Mary, who handed something to her father from her apron pocket. He placed it in the older daughter's outstretched hand. It was a freshly picked, yellow-edged wildflower from the garden.

He closed her hand around it. "You know why we gave you the name Hope, don't you."

It was a statement, not a question. Hope answered, anyway. "Yes, Father. It is to remind us that no matter how dark the night, the sun will rise again in the morning to chase away the shadows."

His smile was weaker now, but his will seemed too strong to let go yet. With the help of his son, Thomas raised himself up and looked into Hope's eyes. "This flower will remind you—as yours did at my most difficult moments—that when your journey is finished, you will return to Mother and me. We will be there to welcome you to a warm hearth."

Thomas lay back on the bed. A shadow suddenly covered the window as if the sun had slipped behind a cloud. An enormous, red-headed face appeared.

Thomas' eyes brightened. "My old friend, it is so nice to see you after so many years."

"We come to pay honor to a giant," remarked Forestmaster in his quietest booming voice.

The children and adults crowded around the window in awe and wonder. It took a few minutes for Hope to calm them. They finally moved aside, allowing Thomas to see Forestmaster clearly. There were a number of giants standing reverently making a wide half-circle in the yard. Hope knew most of the giants from the descriptions given by her father over the years. Those who had come to pay their respects included Earthwatcher, Loamcarver, Threadweaver, Mountainbiter, Needbringer, Bladesmelter, and several others.

Each giant in turn leaned down to the window and shared words of appreciation and honor for her father. There was one conversation she found particularly moving. A smaller giant looked in, his face streaming with tears.

"Horsetender! Thank you for coming. Is it well with you?" Father spoke with an unexpected burst of energy.

"Yes, I have served many years and learned where something worth finding may be found, thank you," replied Horsetender. "I have brought you a poultice that may ease your condition, my friend."

"Do I have to *eat* it or *smell* it?" Father asked with the hint of a smile. The house shook as the giants laughed.

"I am sorry, but this one you will have to eat *and* smell," chuckled Horsetender. He set a small bowl on the windowsill, and the giants backed away.

"None of us like the smell, either," Mountainbiter joked.

Hope helped her father eat a couple of spoonfuls.

Thomas held his breath and swallowed as fast as possible. "That was fouler than I ever remember," he complained, but his voice sounded stronger than it had in many days.

"It is a much stronger poultice," Horsetender said with a compassionate smile. "But unfortunately, you can measure its strength by its foul smell and taste."

"I thank you all for coming. You see, children? The giant people are kind and caring, as should we all strive to be. But I do not encourage any of you to learn the art of making poultice." Thomas winked at Hope as the giants laughed again.

Then one other giant's face appeared at the window. Hope could not mistake the face of Sonspeaker. "My esteemed friend," he said, "you have lived the life of a giant, and our people are blessed by its touch, Thomas Hopegiver. You may meet Worldmaker soon. The meeting will seem familiar, for you have become much like him. It will be a time of great joy and celebration." He looked at Hope. "Do you have the staff?"

"It hangs in a place of honor above the hearth," she replied. "We all know its purpose. Father and Mother taught us well."

"Please fetch it," Sonspeaker said. "I must return it to our Forest Ward. There may be a need for it soon. I sense a change in the weather. A storm is coming. Another may need to walk where your father has walked." He spoke the words with a serious look. "There must always be One, for that is The Way of Things."

"You see, Hope?" Thomas said. "A giant loves to make a good riddle. If you are going to be in their company you must be patient, or you will never learn the whole story. My dear children"—he looked around the room, his energy visibly ebbing—"I have loved you without reservation . . . and you have returned that love tenfold. Go to your labors tomorrow and continue the work of giants . . . for so you have become."

His energy spent, Thomas closed his eyes. His grasp loosened, and his hand fell onto the bed. Hope quickly picked it up and held it close. She bowed her head and said, "You will always be my giant. I love you."

Thomas watched from somewhere above the bed as the scene played out. Sonspeaker, Forestmaster, and the other giants looked up at him and smiled. He turned as he felt his father's hand in his, and they walked side by side once again.

Then his father stopped and gestured ahead with his free hand. Thomas looked. In the distance he saw what appeared to be a field of ripe grain heavy with morning mist. The mist parted and Rachael stood in the field with her arms outstretched to welcome him. He turned to his father, who nodded. Thomas ran to Rachael. He felt young again and lifted her above him, spinning her around. She hugged him tightly and whispered in his ear, "My love, welcome to the Land of Giants." They embraced as only those who have been apart for too long and love so deeply can embrace.

But then, at this most joyous of moments, Rachael gently pulled away. She gazed into his eyes and said, "I see that your work is not yet complete. More is required of you. I will ever be here to give you a warm welcome, but you should return to finish your course."

"How can I leave your side?" Thomas asked, shocked. "I have missed you terribly!"

"My dear, please understand that it must be your choice whether to return or not," Rachael said, compassion in her voice. "You may, of course, decide to stay here."

Thomas hesitated. He felt the same sense of unfinished business calling him back. He wept and held Rachael close. He had always loved their quiet moments together and wished he could stay. But he knew in his heart it was not yet time.

He stepped back with renewed faith. "It will not be long until we shall be together again," he said with difficulty.

"Go, my love. Complete your task and return to my warm hearth and open arms." As she spoke these words, Rachael seemed to recede. Then she disappeared into the mist.

Thomas became aware that he was lying down, but the bed seemed to be bouncing and the sun was warm on his face. It was bright as noonday, and his eyes had not adjusted. He kept them shut and slid his right hand to his side in order to find something sturdy to grasp. His fingers closed around an object lying next to him—the gnarled staff.

Why is this staff lying in my bed? he wondered. *And why is my bed bouncing? I must be dizzy from the high fever.* The sense of rhythmic motion continued. Thomas' eyes adjusted to the bright sunlight, and he opened them.

He lay cradled in Forestmaster's arms, and the giants were moving north.

THE END

If you enjoyed reading about giants in this award winning first book
in the series, the good news is you get to continue your adventures
in the wild world with the remaining two books:

Giants in the Land
Book Two: The Prodigals

Giants in the Land
Book Three: The Cavern of Promise

Glossary of Characters

I HAVE ENJOYED writing about the many rich and interesting characters in this book and feel now that they are old friends. It is hard to say I created these characters because they seemed to walk into my mind with already developed lives of their own.

It occurred to me that it might be helpful to provide a glossary of the characters the reader will meet in this ancient land. Trust me; it was just as interesting and unexpected for me to meet them around every corner as it was for you. Books Two and Three of the series add a number of wonderful, strange, and sometimes dangerous new characters just around the bend. I hope you enjoy the brief summary of how each character fits in the story. I could write volumes on each one but then that would spoil the book for anyone who turns to the glossary first. There is only one sure thing; there are more exciting introductions to come.

The Giants

Bladesmelter: Master Blacksmith of the giants.

Earthwatcher: The giant tasked with monitoring towns from which giants have recently removed. He also serves as companion to a Forest Ward.

Forestmaster: Working companion of Thomas and closest friend. Leader of the Giants mission to the town where Thomas grows up. Husband to Threadweaver.

Healthminder: Physician and healer to the giants.

Herdminder: Leader of the giants who care for the giant cattle, herds and domesticated beasts.

Horsetender: Once rebellious giant befriended by Thomas. He is a master poultice maker.

Loamcarver: Oversees the giant's agricultural production.

Mountainbiter: Sculptor of the giants and responsible for creating and maintaining the passageway over the great barrier. He likes nothing better than to hear or tell an exciting story.

Needbringer: The giant tasked with identifying needs in towns and recommending the extent of the giant response.

Rainbender: Responsible for the extensive irrigation system in the Land of Giants.

Sonspeaker: The Leader of the giant's Grand Council.

Stonebreaker: One of the giants serving Thomas' town. An expert mason known for his work on the town's stockade. Also known as a practical joker.

Threadweaver: Master weaver, clothmaker and leatherworker of the giants. Wife to Forestmaster.

Worldmaker: Deity of the giants. Creator of 'The Way of Things'.

The People

Aiden: The original chosen One of Westhall.

Captain of the Guard: Leader of the guard that protects Thomas' town in his youth.

Hope: Oldest child of Thomas and Rachael. Thomas' inspiration during his lonely journey to find the giants.

Jonathan: Husband to Hope.

Mary: Youngest child of Thomas and Rachael.

Mayor Nimblebone: Mayor of the town in which Thomas lives as a young and middle aged man. He commissions Thomas to go in search of the giants after they have disappeared.

Rachael: Beloved wife of Thomas. Influential leader in town and inspiration to the people. Dies prematurely of a winter disease.

Samuel: Second child and oldest son of Thomas and Rachael.

The Unexpected Visitor: A Forest Ward that Thomas meets on his first journey to find the giants. He gives Thomas advice and a gift.

Thomas: Only person to volunteer to seek out the giants who have disappeared. Husband of Rachael and Father to Hope, Samuel and Mary. Also named by the giants, Thomas Hopegiver.

Thomas Sr: Thomas' father who is tragically killed in a farming accident. He becomes Thomas' inspiration at key points in his journey.

Acknowledgments

THIS STORY WOULD not have been possible if my friend Brad Bertoch had not suggested the original idea in 1997, during a speech he gave as director of the Wayne Brown Institute. Brad has great insight into the needs of businesses as they develop and strive to become self-sufficient. I am grateful for the unintentional planting of the seed for *Giants in the Land.* However, the story is not just about giants and how they impact our lives.

It is about how we continue on once the giants are gone, as they eventually are in one way or another. I therefore must thank those who have been giants in my life. There are too many to mention all of them individually; you know who you are.

To my parents, who have passed on but seem to look in on me from time to time: thank you for believing in me and never giving up helping me to become more than I otherwise might have been.

To my children, each one of you has given my life greater purpose and made it more meaningful than I ever imagined. One of my greatest joys has been to watch each of you step out of the shadow of your older siblings and parents and become your own person. You are, and have always been, my greatest treasure.

To those friends and family who have contributed directly to this work: Alan Peterson; Karin and Chloe Cook; Travis, Shaunna, and Courtney Burbidge; Chelsea Merkley; Colton Riddle; Shauntae Browning; Landon Germaine; Brooke and Jake Cook; and my friends at WinePress and Bookwise Publishing: thank you for the honest and inspiring advice and read-throughs that helped *Giants* come to life the first time around. Also a special thanks to the wonderful people at Deep River Books who saw the beauty of the Giants in the Land series and stepped in to help bring it back to the market with new material.

To the many dear souls who have been there along my path at critical moments. My life has become something worthwhile because of your influence and guidance. You have made all the difference.

Lastly, to my sweetheart, Leah, who ever stands by with love mixed with wise and unreserved counsel: you have the heart and soul of a true giant.

Other Books
by Clark Rich Burbidge

Fiction: Gold Medal Award-Winning Young Adult Trilogy:

StarPassage: Book One – The Relic
StarPassage: Book Two – Heroes and Martyrs
StarPassage: Book Three - Honor and Mercy
StarPassage: Book Four - Cyber Plague

Fiction: Gold Medal Award-Winning Young Adult/Middle Reader Trilogy:

Giants in the Land: Book One – The Way of Things
Giants in the Land: Book Two – The Prodigals
Giants in the Land: Book Three – The Cavern of Promise

Fiction: Gold Medal Award-Winning Family Christmas Picture Book:

A Piece of Silver: A Story of Christ

Non-Fiction Family and Personal:

*Living in the Family Blender:
10 Principles of a Successful Blended Family*

*Life on the Narrow Path: A Mountain Biker's Guide to
Spiritual Growth in Troubled Times*

Websites:

www.starpassagebook.com
www.giantsinthelandbook.com
www.apieceofsilver.com

Like my Facebook page and catch all the news at:

www.facebook.com/clarkrburbidge
www.facebook.com/blendedfamilyproject

www.ingramcontent.com/pod-product-compliance
Lightning Source LLC
Chambersburg PA
CBHW021213160726
47994CB00001B/453